"Sutton! Hey, Lee! H

Lee looked around f
and nodded to the TA w
him. Tall enough to see over the crowd—partially
because he was up front, on the raised platform
for the lecturer—Tony Sanchez was trapped on
the other side of the flow of students.

"What's up?" Lee bulled his way through
his classmates, apologizing without looking at
the people who were nudged aside or had to
stop walking to let him through. "Something
wrong with last semester?" God, he hoped not.
His scholarships were all riding on top grades
and he'd thought he'd hang onto the money for
at least the first full year. There wouldn't be a
second year at all without the scholarships.

"No, it's fine." Tony smiled at him and held
up a hand as he turned to Professor Jenness. "I'll
stop by your office right after my seminar with
Dr. Weild, if that's okay?"

She nodded and gave Lee a curious glance
as if trying to bring his name to mind, but then
merely smiled at him, too, before saying, "Sure,
Tony. See you then." The last of her papers
stuffed into her beaten up leather satchel, she
joined the students leaving the room and was
immediately drawn into a conversation.

"Do you have a free period now?" Tony
asked as he pulled on his jacket. "Can I buy you
a cup of coffee?"

Acquired Tastes
TOP SHELF
An imprint of Torquere Press Publishers
PO Box 2545
Round Rock, TX 78680
Copyright 2009 © by Chris Owen
Cover illustration by Alessia Brio
Published with permission
ISBN: 978-1-60370-854-8, 1-60370-854-5
www.torquerepress.com

**If you enjoyed Acquired Tastes,
you might enjoy these Torquere Press titles:**

A Promise Kept by Stormy Glenn

Bareback by Chris Owen

Becoming Us by Anah Crow and Dianne Fox

Kegs and Dorms by Jane Davitt, Kiernan Kelly, Tory
Temple, and Stephanie Vaughan

Perfect by Julia Talbot

Acquired Tastes

Acquired Tastes
by Chris Owen

romance for the rest of us
www.torquerepress.com

Acquired Tastes

Dedication, Thanks, and Acknowledgements

T his novel is dedicated to Claire, who yelled a very loud "Woo Hoo!" on a busy street when I told her it was finished. It's always nice to be appreciated.

* * *

I wish to thank Addison Albright for the title of this novel, and Carrigan Chantz and Stephanie for the use of their names along with fragments of their personalities. It was far more fun working you into the book than the process had any right to be, and I hope you are both pleased with how you acted in my hands. I think you're both delightful, but I admit to bias. It was a real pleasure working with all three of you, and I thank you for your participation in this singular experience.

~Chris

Acquired Tastes

Chapter One
Brother Mine

Lee Sutton had the wrench and his toolbox with him, and he was prepared to fiddle with sink drains, leaky faucets, or whatever it was that had made Dr. Reed call him, but his mind was still full of the critical essay he'd been working on less than five minutes before. Making the jump from student in full-on work mode to property manager dealing with plumbing issues was a little jarring. Lee had to bury any resentment he had and put on a professional—if not friendly—smile. He really couldn't afford to alienate the residents, thereby making his own life more difficult.

He pressed the doorbell, carefully angling the wrench in his hand away from the door so he wouldn't bang it on the glass window pane. Lee caught a glimpse of himself in the glass and looked away quickly; it was one of those angles that made his deep set eyes look positively evil, too dark and mysterious for comfort. He thought he looked like a hoodlum.

Lee looked around the yard instead while he waited for someone to answer, and hoped that he wouldn't be at Dr. Reed's condo for too long. If it looked like a serious plumbing issue, he would call in a pro instead of spending hours trying to take care of it himself. There were limits to what he was capable of, and also to what was his responsibility—not to mention there were better uses for his time, in Lee's own opinion. Still, it was his job and Dr. Reed couldn't be blamed for his timing. Accidents happened.

It was early evening, just coming on to dusk, and the walk across the property from his little cottage to the U-shaped complex wasn't quite enough time for him to let go of political theory. He was halfway around the building before he realized that sink trouble meant he should go to the back entrance, into the kitchen of Dr. Reed's place, and not to the front door. He backtracked, trying harder to get his mind on the current job and off of comparative politics.

The kitchen door opened, allowing light and warm food smells to waft out; the scents were heavy on tomato and garlic, and it occurred to Lee that he hadn't eaten since lunch. Dr. Reed smiled and nodded at him. "Hey, Lee. Thanks for coming up."

Dr. Reed looked harried but elegant in a dress shirt and silk tie. His dark blond hair was as neatly styled as ever, and his trousers had razor sharp creases. It didn't escape Lee's notice that he would have been able to give a detailed description of what Dr. Reed was wearing, right down to the hand stitching on the cuffs of his shirt. That was only partially due to automatically taking note of what a handsome man was wearing.

"Not a problem, Dr. Reed," Lee assured him, walking in and glancing around. "This is a bad time to have the sink messed up," he added as he set down the toolbox. The stainless steel appliances all gleamed, as did the white tile floor. The counters were covered in serving dishes, plates and bottles of wine, and there were warmers set up on the round wooden table. It looked like a party was going on, but the feast had not yet started. "I'll be as quick as I can, and then get out of your way."

"God, don't worry about it." Dr. Reed rolled his eyes at Lee. "Maybe we can stretch this out long enough that I'll be able to eat dinner and then hustle this crowd to the event, skipping the drawn- out cocktail hour. Come on, it's the upstairs sink, in the master bath. I would have let it go until morning, but it's a guest's item. Bernie dropped an earring."

That didn't sound too bad. Lee picked up the toolbox again. "Big night?" Maybe Dr. Reed was getting an award or something and Lee should offer his congratulations.

"For some. Do you need help carrying anything?" Dr. Reed smiled at him when Lee shook his head, then glanced at the door to the rest of the living space. His brow furrowed, making his expression more exasperated than pleased or amused. "It's just a company function to celebrate the new CFO, but it's my turn to host the department's pre-dinner drinks. We don't get out much, and a few of us tend to go all out when we get the chance."

"Well, you look just fine." Lee couldn't have cared less who dressed up, drank too much, went all out or stayed home to read a book. He blinked, surprised to find that he'd spoken his thought out loud, and willed himself not to blush or make things worse with a stammering retraction.

A roar of laughter from the other room seemed to startle Dr. Reed into motion. "Um, this way. I think Bernie tried to get it out. I have no idea what she did, honestly."

Lee lifted his chin in acknowledgement and didn't roll his eyes. Bernie might be a ditz or she might not be, but she was a friend of Dr. Reed's and that meant Lee had to be polite, even if she'd taken the stopper mechanism out and made a mess of it. "I'll take a look; no trouble at all. I might have to take the trap off from underneath, though, so if you have a bucket that'd be really handy."

"Sure." Dr. Reed changed direction and crossed to a broom closet beside the pantry. He got out a bucket, then headed out of the kitchen. "I'll show you up; she's still up there, I think."

They walked through the dining room, the table covered in linens but not yet set with plates or crystal, and around the corner into a living room full of people. At least half a dozen guests, perhaps a few more, were sitting or standing around the room.

They were all dressed for something fancy, the ladies in long gowns and the men in suits; one man was in a tux, complete with an expertly knotted bow tie that was definitely not a clip-on. Lee tried very hard to ignore the fact that his entire outfit probably didn't cost as much as Dr. Reed's shirt. Worse than knowing that little fact, though, was that Lee was wearing his good clothes, too, since he'd had a meeting with his advisor in the afternoon. His best clothes, and he couldn't even come close to being as neatly dressed as these people.

He was suddenly acutely aware of the tools in his hand and that the conversation had come to a sudden halt. He resisted the urge to pat his hair; it was dark and messy, and that was just the way it was.

"I'll be right back," Dr. Reed said cheerfully to his guests, clearly unaware of anything Lee might be thinking. He headed up the stairs, one hand resting lightly on the railing. "Help yourself to refills if you need them, okay?"

The man in the tuxedo lifted his glass to Lee and said, "Good luck, son."

"Am I going to need it?" Lee quietly asked Dr. Reed as

they turned at the landing.

"Well, that was Bernie's husband, so yes." Dr. Reed gave him a quick smile. "You're just her type."

As Bernie's husband looked like he was in his mid-fifties, had a paunch and a receding hairline, Lee took the warning and the comment to heart. "I can pretty much promise she's not my type."

"I'll take care of it." Dr. Reed glanced at him as he led the way down the hall. "She's actually pretty easy to manage. She merely operates on the base assumption that you're fascinated by what she's fascinated by, and if she wants something it's hers. It's like she never left kindergarten in some ways. Feigned interest can accomplish a lot."

"Oh." Lee couldn't help the twist of his lips. "She's one of those."

"She is indeed." Dr. Reed, thankfully, didn't seem to mind that Lee was already unimpressed with the lady who needed help retrieving her jewelry.

"I'll be as quick as I can."

"I believe you." Dr. Reed let him into the master bedroom through two French doors. "Bernadette, he's here, dear. All will be well."

The room was large, as Lee knew it would be. He hadn't been in Dr. Reed's upper level before, his previous calls to the condo being confined to the kitchen and the crawl space under the building, but it was one of the two corner units in the complex and Lee had been in the other. The two units had more windows than the rest, a very large master suite, and two smaller bedrooms on the second floor. Given the size of the room, Lee was unsurprised to find the four-poster king-sized bed and heavy wooden dressers. It was an open and bright space, but very masculine in terms of color and fabric. He would have decorated in much the same way, given a huge increase in his budget.

Lee's own room was a collection of what was on sale when he needed sheets and towels, but then, he wasn't a PhD yet. Dr. Reed was and had been for a few years.

A blonde woman sat perched on the end of the bed, her feet dangling and one shoe on the floor while the other shoe hung precariously from her toes. She was dressed as the other women were, in satin or silk, though she was in pale pink and had a lot more ruffles to her skirt. "Thank goodness," she said in a curiously pitched voice, both soft and high. "I wouldn't have been able to leave without it, you know."

"It's an earring?" Lee asked her. He reached out and took the bucket from Dr. Reed, already moving toward the bathroom.

"Yes, diamonds." She got off the bed and held onto the post while she got her shoes back on. "I'll help."

Lee turned away from her so she couldn't see his face and rolled his eyes. "That's okay, Miss. I can handle it on my own."

Dr. Reed intercepted Bernie and stopped her protests simply by speaking louder than she did. "It's the sink on the right, Lee," he said. "I think Bernie and I will stay here, out of your way."

"Speak for yourself, Joey. I'm going to go and watch this lovely man save my diamonds." She sounded determined and very sure of herself. She lifted her chin high and her mouth curled saucily at one corner as she breezed past Dr. Reed and into the bathroom, her heels clicking on the tiles.

Lee did his best to ignore her as she leaned on the counter, her fingers curled around the edge. Her nails were painted the same shiny pink as her dress, and when she leaned down to watch him clear out the area under the sink, Lee had to hope that she wasn't going to fall out of her dress.

"You're awfully kind to come rushing over with your big wrench," she said into his ear, almost purring, her breath warm on the side of his face.

"Oh, for the love of God." Dr. Reed didn't bother hiding his annoyance. "Bernie. Let the man work, okay?"

"He's fine," she said, brushing Dr. Reed off and laughing. The dress must have been made of Teflon the way words, mood, and attitude were deflected away from her. "He's a big boy, and I'm sure he can take care of himself. Joey, darling, why don't you run along and see to the others?"

"Oh, I don't think so."

Getting a flashlight from his tool box, Lee pretended he couldn't hear the banter. Instead, he did his job and checked to make sure that the earring wasn't merely caught in the drain, but no matter how he shone his light down there, there was no sparkle at all.

"You're so attractive when you glare at me like that, Joey," Bernie said with a laugh that was a lot deeper than her speaking voice. "If you would dress down a bit you'd even be worth the work it would take to turn your head."

Dr. Reed snorted and Lee decided it would be best to get out of their direct line of sight, so he bent and opened the vanity doors under the sink. While Dr. Reed talked to Bernie and was put off once again, Lee started to move things out of the cupboard. Cleaning supplies, a plunger, four rolls of toilet paper and a cardboard box that had a few odd things in it like a soap dish and a plastic cup were set aside, and then he put the bucket in under the U-bend sink trap.

"I don't blame you for calling him," Bernie was saying in a loud stage whisper to Dr. Reed. "He clearly knows what he's doing and you might have gotten your shirt dirty. Plus, he has a great ass."

"Don't you dare touch him."

"Spoilsport."

Dr. Reed sighed. Loudly. "Bernie. Go downstairs and sit next to your husband. Tell him I said you're not allowed to have any more gimlets."

She huffed, and in the relative safety of having his head stuck in a cupboard, Lee rolled his eyes for what felt like the ninth time. Maybe he could make a lot of noise and drown her out while he got the trap off the drain pipe.

"Why are you so cranky tonight?" she was saying.

"Because you're being stubborn and rude." Joey didn't sound mad, Lee noted absently. Actually, he sounded like they had this conversation on a fairly regular basis.

Lee worked at the pipe, banged his elbow, and kept on going. He wasn't coming out until they either left the bathroom or he had the earring. Determined, he opened the cleaning valve at the bottom of the bend, but all that came out was water; if there was an earring in there, it was being stubborn.

Putting the cap back on, Lee started to unscrew the brackets on either side of the trap, inwardly lamenting his lot in life for the evening. His world was usually pretty peaceful between school, living alone, and the quiet solitude of his job. He liked it that way. He supposed he should be grateful that these interruptions—the ones that included forward house guests—were very few and far between. It was a lot easier to simply remain under the sink and pretend they weren't there.

Dr. Reed succeeded in moving Bernie out of the bathroom, despite her vocal pouting about it. Lee could hear them talking in the main part of the bedroom and from the tone of the conversation, they eventually moved on to something having to do with Dr. Reed's job. It didn't sound salacious at all, and the words that got through to Lee despite his best efforts at ignoring them all sounded like business. The way the two of them could go from acting one way and then right into its direct opposite made Lee wonder about where their true personalities lay. Not that it mattered, he supposed. He was the help and that was all.

With a tug and some awkward maneuvering, Lee managed to get the sink trap off. His hand came down, hitting the rim of the bucket and he dropped the trap right in as he fell backward onto his butt.

"Oh!" Bernie leaned in the door, apparently able to move a lot faster than Dr. Reed despite the high heeled shoes. "Did you hurt yourself?" Again, she was about to lose her dress as she made to help him up.

Afraid that if he took the offered hand he would wind up with a lap full of Bernie, Lee shook his head and kept his hands to himself. "No." He rolled slightly and steadied himself, then reached into the bucket and upended the trap as the drain continued to drip from both newly opened sides. "I'm fine."

"Bernie, please let him work," Dr. Reed said, not sounding as if he had much hope. Lee glanced up to see him looking at the ceiling, his mouth quirked in a resigned smile.

"It's fine." Lee shook the trap and something fell out with a wet plop. He shone the light into the bucket and made a face. "Yuck."

"Is it ruined?"

"Nothing ruins diamonds," Lee said mildly. He shook the curved pipe again and this time something rattled and then fell out. Thankfully, it missed the blob. "One earring, for sure. Hang on a moment." He fit the trap back into place and tightened it back up, then backed out of the cupboard with the bucket in hand.

Standing, he watched both Bernie's and Dr. Reed's reflections in the mirror as he ran the water and rinsed off the earring. Bernie was suddenly only looking at his hands, and Dr. Reed seemed to be very interested in the state of the calcium and lime build up on his shower walls.

"Here you go," Lee said as he patted water off the earring with a hand towel and then held it out to Bernie. "As good as new, I hope."

She made a sound that could only be described as a squeal and took a step forward, her arms lifting. Lee took an instinctive step back to ward off the incoming hug and possibly a kiss, but the counter was there and he was trapped. His face must have shown something, however, because she stopped herself and held out a hand to take the earring. "What's wrong?" she asked, her glance sliding over to Dr. Reed. "Are you like him? Girls aren't good enough for you?"

Dr. Reed's eyes narrowed. "Say thank you, Bernie, and go downstairs. Put your earring in and make sure it doesn't fall down another drain."

"Touchy. I should've known." She leaned over the counter and took her time putting the earring in, then appeared to pointedly ignore them both while she adjusted her dress and checked her makeup. Without another word she turned and walked from the room, her hips swaying.

"Bitch," Dr. Reed said under his breath. "I'll be right back, Lee. I need to go put out a fire, but I'll be back to apologize properly in just a moment."

Lee shook his head. "There's no need, Dr. Reed. You didn't do anything."

"Joey. I'll be right back."

Shrugging, Lee started putting things away. As a name, Joey didn't really seem to suit Dr. Reed, but his parents certainly couldn't have been expected to know that he'd grow up into a self-possessed, good-looking man with sharp brown eyes and perfect hair, educated and sophisticated. He was far more a Joseph or even a Joe than a Joey.

With everything back where it was supposed to be, Lee put the flashlight and wrench in his tool box and stood up once more. He'd deal with the lump of disgusting hair and soap residue to make sure nothing else was lost in there, then see if he could sneak out before Joey Reed came back to make an unnecessary apology. There was still a paper waiting for Lee's attention, and if he finished up by midnight or so he might even have time for a beer before he fell asleep. Weekend fun had taken on a whole new meaning as a PhD candidate than it had had when he was doing his undergraduate work. Long gone were the days of all night parties and putting off the homework until Sunday afternoon.

Lee left the glob in the bucket and ran a few inches of water in with it, then shook things around a little to loosen the mess. When it started to come apart he put more water in and started poking it, trying not to be too grossed out. Sure enough, there was a solid bit there. "Damn it." Muttering to himself Lee put even more water in the bucket and poked at the mess until the object came free. "Gotcha."

He'd have to take the bucket with him to get rid of the mess properly, but he was sure that Dr. Reed wouldn't mind, given the circumstances. He'd just leave the cleaned out bucket on the back step in the morning. Setting the bucket aside, Lee took what turned out to be a pin of some kind and rinsed it off in the sink, just as he'd done with Bernie's earring. It wasn't until he was wiping it dry on the hand towel that he actually looked at it.

Lee wasn't sure how long he stood there, staring, before Dr. Reed came back.

"Lee? Lee, are you okay? What's wrong?" Dr. Reed stood close to him, one hand on Lee's arm, like he thought perhaps Lee was going to fall over.

Lee shook his head minutely, his gaze so fixed on the unexpected pin that he wasn't sure he'd ever be able to look away. He had never thought, not even once, that he'd see a pin like that again; not in a new city, at a new school, a new home. The chills from the shock were turning liquid smooth under Dr. Reed's hand. "I'm fine," Lee heard himself say. "Just fine."

Dr. Reed clearly didn't believe him and was saying exactly that, but Lee was looking at the pin, turning it around in his fingers. The gold had been warmed by the water he'd washed it in, pleasant to hold. It was a triangular lapel pin, elegant and small, its matte face etched on the three sides with a spear, an arrow and a javelin. That was all. It was the mark of TCF, a secret society.

It was the one way that Lee could know a brother.

Lee could picture his own pin, across the yard in his cottage, in the small jewelry box in the top drawer of his dresser. His was between his father's wedding band and his grandfather's pocket watch.

Holding the pin out to Dr. Reed on the flat of his palm and still looking only at it, Lee whispered, "Achilles and Patrocles, Alexander and Hephaestion. Heroes in life, legends in death."

A heavy near-silence took over the ringing in his ears, but Lee could feel every thump and whoosh of his heartbeat.

Dr. Reed didn't move away from him but he managed, somehow, to close the bathroom door. The already muted sounds of the house party vanished and they were insulated from the world, encapsulated in a bathroom, of all places. Never before had a meeting of TCF had less glamorous surroundings. "What did you say?"

With great effort Lee made himself look up and

meet Dr. Reed's equally stunned expression. He'd had a moment of doubt when Dr. Reed didn't immediately reply—what if the pin had been lost by the last owner of the condo?—but the look in Dr. Reed's eyes was truth. "You heard me." They were both whispering, but in Lee's case it was a matter of physical necessity; his throat felt raw, like he'd been yelling or crying for hours.

Dr. Reed's fingers shook as he took the pin from Lee's palm. His mouth opened and closed, then opened again as he looked at the face of it, his eyes distant. "Bones mixed," he said softly. "One soul in two bodies. The Brotherhood of Leuce."

Lee nodded and they finished together, "Beloved, inspired, cherished and protected. The Chosen Family."

There was a moment of silence so intense that Lee thought perhaps even his heartbeat was stilled. "You lost your pin." His voice sounded constricted.

"Lee." Dr. Reed moved, his arms slipping around Lee and hugging him tight, laughing in delight as if he'd found a long lost brother.

Lee had to admit to himself that, in fact, Joey had. The hesitation Lee felt was real, but he pushed it aside quickly and hugged Dr. Reed back, just as fiercely, his arms starting to tingle as adrenaline rushed through his body. Absurdly, his only real thought was that he was really going to have to call Dr. Reed Joey, now.

"I had no idea you went to CSUC. I thought you were at Legacy." Joey didn't even let him go, just backed up enough to let there be a little bit of air between them even though their arms were looped around each other. He was smiling widely, his whole face alive and animated.

"I am, for my doctorate." Lee moved his hands to Joey's hips, unsure what else to do with them. "But I was at CSUC for my BA. Class of '02."

"I was '97." Joey finally let him go, but looked reluctant

to do it. "God, we need to sit down and talk. I bet I know your Senior. I must, really. He would have been, uh, in the class of '99."

Lee nodded, "I think so, yes." He had no idea; every single memory was trying to rise to the surface at once, and details were sliding together, just out of reach. He couldn't do this, not right then. Not in a bathroom, with a wrench in his hand and a deadline for his advisor. Not when Joey was every inch Dr. Reed, in his hand-tailored shirt. Lee shook his head and tried to back away subtly. "Later. We will later. You have a house full of people and I need to get back to work."

He wasn't sure if he really wanted to stand around the master bath while Joey started listing off names of The Chosen Family. The family tree could get complicated at the best of times and Lee's brain was completely unfocused, only one thing clear: a brother in the complex. One of the residents, a research scientist.

He wasn't ready for this. Not one bit. Lee liked his life to be nice and smooth and predictable; a sudden friendship with a neighbor, while nice, wasn't something that Lee had bargained for. This needed some thinking.

"I have to go."

Joey looked disappointed and frustrated by reality. "They're going to come looking for me, anyway. But you and I are going to sit down very soon and catch up." He smiled hopefully, his eyes big and lit up like a child's, shining with hope and excitement.

If it had been anyone but a brother, Lee would have blown him off without thinking twice. But Joey was family and once upon a time Lee had made promises that he still believed in. "Of course." He nodded, serious. "Soon."

Looking pleased, Joey leaned forward and kissed Lee's cheek. "You are like me," he whispered happily. "Gay, smart, decent. A brother and all that it means."

Lee's heart skipped a beat and he wasn't sure if it was because of how untrue that was or how true he wanted it to be. Being a brother had been the most amazing thing in his life; graduating and putting that behind him had been hard. Opening up to it again would be... something to think about much later in the night. "We'll talk soon," he said again numbly.

Chapter Two
The Invitation

Lee's first class after the Christmas break of his freshman year at CSUC was Psych 102. It was held on Monday morning at ten, and Lee was grateful that the room wasn't too warm; he hadn't had time for his morning caffeine, and psychology wasn't interesting enough to keep him completely awake in a room warmed by over a hundred other students.

There were too many electives to fill up the freshmen year, in Lee's opinion.

Because it was the first class of the new term, they didn't do a lot other than get the syllabus, confirm that they'd taken and passed Psych 101, and were in the right room at the right time. The professor, a woman named Jenness, gave them a fast review of the highlights from before the holiday break, and they didn't quite manage to fill the fifty-five minute period. Professor Jenness wasn't interested in holding them and with a wave at the board where she'd written their assigned reading for the next class, she released them early.

Lee joined the rest of the throng in filing out of the room, his mind already moving ahead to what he had to

24

do that afternoon. He had to buy some food—hopefully the produce would be marked down and he could get some bananas—and he'd have to phone his grandmother before he went to work, to make sure she'd remembered to pay the electric bill on time. The last thing either of them needed was for her to lose power in January.

"Sutton! Hey, Lee! Hang on a second."

Lee looked around for the owner of the voice and nodded to the TA who was waving a hand at him. Tall enough to see over the crowd—partially because he was up front, on the raised platform for the lecturer—Tony Sanchez was trapped on the other side of the flow of students.

"What's up?" Lee bulled his way through his classmates, apologizing without looking at the people who were nudged aside or had to stop walking to let him through. "Something wrong with last semester?" God, he hoped not. His scholarships were all riding on top grades and he'd thought he'd hang onto the money for at least the first full year. There wouldn't be a second year at all without the scholarships.

"No, it's fine." Tony smiled at him and held up a hand as he turned to Professor Jenness. "I'll stop by your office right after my seminar with Dr. Weild, if that's okay?"

She nodded and gave Lee a curious glance as if trying to bring his name to mind, but then merely smiled at him, too, before saying, "Sure, Tony. See you then." The last of her papers stuffed into her beaten up leather satchel, she joined the students leaving the room and was immediately drawn into a conversation.

"Do you have a free period now?" Tony asked as he pulled on his jacket. "Can I buy you a cup of coffee?"

Lee shrugged one shoulder and nodded. He and Tony weren't precisely strangers, but he hadn't thought of them as even acquaintances. They'd had perhaps two conversations that weren't about the course at parties earlier in the school year. Lee would have called Tony a friend of a friend, if he'd been asked for anything more specific than teacher assistant. "I won't turn down free coffee."

"Good enough." Tony gave him a friendly smile, picked up his books, and they left.

The closest place for coffee was actually off campus, across the street from the primary humanities building. They mixed in with students, office workers and at least one professor, glad that the line moved quickly. It was prime time for a mid-morning break and the shop was jammed.

"Want a muffin?" Tony reached across Lee and grabbed a banana, a muffin, and a cookie. "I didn't have breakfast yet. Grab one, if you want."

Hesitating only long enough to remember the lack of food in his cupboard, Lee nodded and picked out a bran muffin to go with his coffee. "Thanks."

"No problem. How was your holiday?" Tony kept smiling at Lee, his gaze friendly.

Lee was starting to wonder if this was a date, but it didn't actually feel like it. Tony wasn't touching, wasn't coming close to touching at all, and he wasn't eyeing Lee up like he was cruising. He was just being nice. For no particular reason. "Um, good." Lee looked at the girl pouring coffee and said, "Large, thanks."

"Flavor? Whip?"

"No, just a large coffee. Thanks."

She looked mildly confused but dutifully poured coffee into a large paper cup and then held it out to him. "Large. To go. With nothing but coffee."

Lee took it and nodded his approval, then rolled his eyes at Tony.

"It's okay," Tony said in confidential tones as he

leaned across the counter to her. "I'll make it better. Give me a skinny cap with a double shot and two pumps of raspberry."

"That's disgusting," Lee said before he could help himself. "Oh, God. Sorry."

Tony just laughed, though. Really laughed, his eyes closing and his nose wrinkling up at the bridge. "It is, actually. I'm trying to give up coffee and I thought this might help." He paid for everything and they went outside, since there were no tables left inside at all.

"Where to?" Lee asked. He adjusted his backpack and held the coffee in both hands, keeping his fingers warm.

"Let's walk toward the main library," Tony suggested. "I have to photocopy a bunch of stuff. We can talk on the way."

"Sure." Lee looked at him, not moving. "About what?"

"Mmm." Tony sipped his coffee and started walking, forcing Lee to keep up. "Do you know anything about secret societies?"

Lee thought about that as he fought to get his sunglasses out of his pocket. "You mean like the Freemasons?"

"No, I mean actual secret societies. Ones that are still secret, or at the very least have a secret membership. Masons practically carry signs, these days."

Sunglasses on, Lee stopped squinting but sighed as the steam from his coffee immediately fogged them up when he took a sip from his cup. "Well, I know that the NSA was a secret at one point. And I know about the Skull and Bones thing at Yale. Other than that, not much. Why?"

Tony tried to peel his banana as they walked, but with his coffee in his hand he was making a mess of it. "Do you think that secrets can actually be kept by a large amount of people over a long length of time?"

Lee watched him fight with the banana and walked

slowly. There weren't a lot of people on the sidewalk, and no one was waiting to cross back to campus with them at the light. "I suppose so. I mean, state secrets are kept, people run covert operations, there's whole agencies of the government that depend upon secrets—like the NSA. Want me to hold your coffee?" His muffin was safely in his jacket pocket, out of sight. He hoped Tony wouldn't ask about it; Lee could have it for lunch and save himself the four dollars for another meal, though he'd be nearly ravenous by supper.

Tony passed it to him, the light changed, and they walked across the street as Tony got his banana peeled. "There's one here, at CSUC," Tony said as he took back his coffee cup. "I think it would be a good place for you."

It took Lee a few seconds to process the statement. "Right. Because I've always wanted to join a cult." Besides, Lee wouldn't join any club that would have him, as the old joke said.

Tony winked at him and kept walking, following the sidewalk until it turned into a pathway across one of the campus lawns. "No, seriously. Not a cult, I promise. Just a group here on campus with a special focus. It's small, but it's got a long history."

Lee looked at him, disbelieving. "Come on. Secret societies kind of went out of vogue years ago, didn't they? Unless fraternities prancing around in the dark and making freshmen drink beer filtered through underwear counts."

"You really need to watch a lot less television." Tony rolled his eyes and kept walking, but he didn't seem too bothered by Lee's skepticism. "It was started in the 1950's by four men, and it's been going on ever since. It's different from a fraternity, a lot more focused on the time we spend together here at school, rather than making connections for after graduation. Fraternities keep their contacts after graduation and build in a way of using those contacts later in life; we're all about the four years you spend in school."

"Uh-huh." Lee drank his rapidly cooling coffee and walked with him, slightly bemused. "And you think this society would be up my alley?"

"I do." Tony stopped walking, abruptly enough that Lee took an extra step and had to turn around to face him. "If you only knew what a compliment I was paying you by even having this conversation..." Tony grinned suddenly. "Now I know what Nassim meant when he talked to me. Okay, come here." He stepped off the pathway and moved purposefully to one of the many wooden benches scattered all over campus.

"Who's Nassim?" Lee asked, sitting down beside Tony and swinging his bag to the ground, making sure he didn't squish the muffin in his pocket. The bench was chilly, but not as cold as one of the old fashioned stone benches would have been. Lee figured he should be grateful that there wasn't snow, really. For some reason he assumed that this conversation was taking place outside for a definite purpose, and that if they were to go inside there would be too many ears around that Tony wanted to avoid.

Secret societies tended to like to keep their secrets. Lee knew that much, but was hardly proud of the limited brain power it took to put the conclusion together. Their secrets probably tended to be about lame things like who was sleeping with whom, and whose family was actually evading income tax laws. It was all based on privilege and Lee was hardly a child of means. Still. Tony was probably aware of that, and yet, here he was.

Tony made himself comfortable and took his time answering. "Nassim was the guy that brought me in," he said with a smile. "He told me that the hardest part wasn't trying to decide who to invite, but trying to find the words. Now I see what he meant. I could give you a big run around about what we do, and how we need you, how we can help you, but it would be easier for me to just tell you what he told me."

"Easier for you." Lee wasn't sure, but that had the ring of a short cut to it, and he hated not being able to tell if it was a bad thing to short cut or something that would make life a lot easier.

"Hell, yes," Tony said with a laugh. "I'm walking a very fine line here. I have to tell you the truth, I can't lie to you at all, but I can't give away any big secrets. So I'm just going to tell you what he told me that finally made me say, 'this guy isn't crazy, he has something to offer me.' What he said that convinced me to take a step into a mystery."

"Okay." Lee finished his coffee and waited patiently. This was by far the most bizarre conversation he had had in weeks, and that included a very protracted conversation with his grandmother about Christmas elves. "I'm here to listen. Well, for at least another half hour." Listening couldn't hurt anything.

Tony took a deep breath. "It won't take that long, I wouldn't think. Okay, here's the thing." He looked at Lee, his face serious. "In order for a person to become a member of our society, he must demonstrate certain qualities. He must have integrity, intelligence, self-discipline, and honor. For me to even consider talking to you about joining us, I must've already seen this in you. Therefore, I already know that you won't go around campus telling people about the society. In essence, in order to be the kind of man we would like to include, you're already worthy of trust. Do you see what I'm saying?"

Lee nodded slowly. "I think so, yes. I do have a question, though."

"Sure."

"How do you know I'm all that?" Lee couldn't help but grin. "Seriously, we've had only a handful of conversations. If that. How can you be so sure that I'm all that noble?" Even if it did sound nice and make his belly warm.

"It's a valid question." Tony looked him in the eye, and he wasn't smiling. "I asked around, I talked to you. I pay attention in your psych class and saw you do the same. No man is an island, Lee. I made it my business to find out."

Lee wasn't sure if that was disturbing or not. "So you think I'm worthy of trust. What else do you know?"

Tony did smile then, the corners of his mouth twitching. "I know you study too much. I know that you work a lot of hours at two jobs. And I know that you don't go out that often."

"Is that what makes me trustworthy?"

"No," Tony said with a laugh. "That's what makes me think you need us."

Lee rolled his eyes. "Okay, tell me. Do you need some kind of promise that I won't go blabbing?"

"No, that's what I was just saying." Tony shrugged a shoulder at him. "I'm asking you because you're the kind of guy who wouldn't go blabbing. See what I mean? If you were the type of guy who'd make a mess of this, I wouldn't be here."

Lee nibbled at the inside of his lip, a bad habit that he never noticed until it was too late and he was in pain. "Has anyone ever told?"

"Nope. Not that's in the record books, anyway. So don't go making me the first one to make a bad choice of who to invite in, okay?"

Lee smiled. "Okay. I'll do my best to keep from running around all over campus telling everyone my TA for Intro

Psych is in a secret club."

"I appreciate that." Tony flashed him a smile and then looked around them again, pausing for a moment. "In the mid 1950's, four young men came together with an idea of supporting and protecting each other while they completed their degrees here. They were from different towns, different states, but found in each other a sense of belonging and affection. They were also given to a bit of high drama and liked the idea of ritual, plus they thought they were very clever."

Lee raised an eyebrow. "They weren't clever?"

"Oh, yes, they were clever." Tony smiled and nodded a little bit. "They made up a bunch of stuff I can tell you about later, then you can share in the amusement. Here's a free bit of advice, though. Being clever and trying to show that you're clever are two very different things. If you try to show it off, you make things complicated for decades."

"I see," Lee said, not seeing at all. "I'll write that down somewhere."

"Sure. Where was I?"

"Four guys made up a secret society in a clever way."

"Right." Tony nodded. "They did. They spent the next couple of years very carefully expanding their group, refining it to be what they needed, what they wanted, and making the first rules." He shifted on the bench, turning to face Lee and leaning in a little. "I can't tell you all the rules; there's a lot I have to keep from you right now. But I can tell you some of it, if you're interested. This would be a good time for you to walk away, if you're not."

Lee looked at his empty coffee cup and studied a tear in the plastic lid. He was curious, of course—how could someone be invited to join a secret society, be told that he was an honorable and intelligent man, and not be curious? He tried his best to put that aside and to truly consider what Tony was asking, though, tried to be something more than an eighteen year old kid leaping at a chance for immediate gratification.

Could he keep a secret? Of course. Lee was very good at keeping secrets, he knew that already. But could he blindly walk into a situation and promise to keep quiet about things he didn't have any awareness of? Could he essentially promise allegiance to a group on the word of one man, fully knowing that he would know very little more than he already did before the last chance to walk away came? The real question, of course, was if he believed what Tony was telling him.

A group started by four men, decades ago, to support and protect.

"Is this a gay thing?" Lee didn't think it was a huge leap to make, given that he hadn't exactly gone out of his way to hide his tastes and he'd actually met Tony's boyfriend at one of the parties where they'd talked.

Tony nodded once. "It is." His tone was calm and even, his eyes unblinking.

"But not like any other GLBT group, I take it." Lee looked up and then around them, taking in the clear blue sky, the trees bare in the crisp air.

"No. Not like that." Tony's voice dropped and grew even more serious than it had been and he didn't rush his words. Calmly, in measured and precise diction, he said, "Four men per year. Sixteen men on campus at a given time, max. People you can count on, rely on, trust. For anything at all. When you need to talk about the straight guy you've fallen in love with, you will have brothers. When you need to talk about school, your parents, what you saw in a movie, how you're going to get on with your life when you graduate. Fifteen guys you can talk to, knowing they'll keep your secrets, knowing that you don't have to preface any conversation with disclaimers based on who you want to mack on. Guys you know who are just like you—smart, discreet, scrupulous. Support and protect."

Lee felt his breath go still in his chest. It wasn't that he didn't have friends, and it wasn't that he was in need of people to confide in; but Tony's passion, the depth of his belief in those men and the power of feelings was effective. He licked his lower lip and tried to keep himself from getting swept up in Tony's convictions. "Secret passwords? Masks?"

Tony grinned, his entire body relaxing as he sat back. "That and more. No secret handshake, though. Sorry."

"What would I have to do?" It wasn't like he could pay any kind of membership dues.

"Well, we have actual meetings once a month but it's more or less expected that you keep Sunday afternoons for us. We all hang out at a place—study, talk, shoot pool, watch TV. Just be together. You can't be pledged to a fraternity or anything like it—you'll have to make vows and we know that fraternities ask some of the same things. We need to know where your loyalties are: to us. That's why we wait until after Christmas to issue invitations to a freshman, so we know if they're rushing a frat or not."

Lee snorted. He'd taken a look at two fraternities and decided they weren't for him. "What if I have to work on a Sunday afternoon?"

"Then you have to work." Tony shrugged. "We would just like it if you managed to come as often as you're able. Oh, and we don't use the Fa—the group as a pick up farm. While we don't get in a twist about members dating each other and actually trying to have a relationship, we really, really discourage sleeping around within the group. This isn't a sex club."

Lee gave him a long look. "Has it been an issue?"

"Not in a long time, but it was for a while." Tony

waved it off. "History has a way of cycling. There've been periods where we had less than sixteen members because of war, guys off in Vietnam or the Gulf. There was a horrible spell of funerals for past members, in the eighties—for obvious reasons. And every once in a while a group relaxes expectations and there's a lot of sex. The resulting fallout and hurt feelings causes the rules to tighten up again."

"And you're in a tight period."

"We're about due for a relaxed one." Tony winked at him. "But we're trying not to let it happen. So. Harper Lee Sutton, you're invited to meet with us this coming Saturday night at eight p.m.. I'll need an answer pretty much immediately."

"How the hell did you find out my full name?" Lee shook his head and raised his hand at the same time. "Never mind. Teacher Assistant." He stood up and picked up his backpack. "You know where I live?"

"I do." Tony didn't get up, but tilted his head, face full of sunlight as he looked at Lee. "I'll need to come and get you Saturday, if you're coming. The meeting place is secret and you'll be blindfolded. You'll be told where you are during the ceremony, or on your way out, after." He squinted, his hand coming up to shield his eyes. "So. You'll be a brother. Yes?"

Lee looked around the campus and weighed the choice. There wasn't much to think about, really. "Yes." He nodded and offered Tony his hand. "I think I'd like that."

Chapter Three
Straight Talk

Lee carried the bucket from Joey Reed's bathroom back to his bungalow, holding onto the handle so tightly that his fingernails dug into the palm of his hand.

He thought Bernie's husband had made an attempt to say thank you—certainly someone had been talking to Lee as he made his way down the stairs, through the house and out through the kitchen—but he didn't pause to find out. Conversation with anyone was completely beyond him. Thankfully, Joey's return had spurred a conversation with the guests and Lee had merely walked out.

Night had completely fallen by the time he left, and the light from Joey's kitchen window cast an orange rectangle on his patio. After that splash of light were more, one after another from each of the units, making a mutated and symmetrical yellow brick road through the central courtyard and past the swimming pool, ending in a well of darkness that hid his own home.

Lee walked as if he were on autopilot, the bucket held out from his body to avoid any splashing. Without thinking about it, he even paused to make sure the skimmer was running in the pool just like he did every time he passed by. He made his way through the dark, across the lawn and around the edge of his house, muscle memory and sheer habit getting him home.

The buzzing and clattering in his head was starting to die down a little, the night air clearing his mind. He was still stunned, but the mental traffic jam was becoming less like blaring horns and more like a roll call. Names were flooding back, snatches of memories showing a huge room with couches, tables, a cluster of easy chairs. The sound of his own voice repeating a chant of "oh, my God," over and over was mingling with the click of pool cues hitting balls and guys laughing while they went over notes for assorted final exams. He could hear rain hitting the glass windows that made up one entire exterior wall, feel the closeness of being inside with his brothers on gray, autumn days.

He went in through his dark kitchen and put the bucket in the sink, then went right to his bedroom before turning on any lights.

Loose change and receipts cluttered the top of his dresser, along with keys for various places on campus and for the collection of units he tended. Those were all labeled, though, and in an open glass container with Meadowlark Court etched on the side. A wooden bowl was full of random objects and match books, and under it was a large and shiny jewelry case that he'd been given by a well-meaning ex-boyfriend. There wasn't any jewelry in it; that was where Lee kept important things like favorite pens that needed refills and warranty cards that came with electronics.

Ignoring everything on the dresser, Lee opened the top drawer and got out his real treasures. Safely kept in the small wooden jewelry box his grandmother had left to him, only six things were worthy of being prized. For a long moment he merely held the box, and then he went to sit on the edge of his unmade bed, by the bedside lamp.

The hinges were stiff when he lifted the lid, but they always had been; he was used to it and didn't even notice the slight creaking sound they made anymore.

It was still there, of course. The pin sat on red velvet, next to a house key and between the ring and the watch, all four items shining in the light. In a silk bag in a corner was his mother's wedding ring, and his grandmother's, kept apart from the rest because his grandmother had told him to keep them that way, as she'd done. He didn't know why, he merely followed her wishes. As far as he knew, his grandfather had never had a wedding band.

Lee took out his pin and held it for a moment or two, his fingers tracing the triangle of ancient Greek weapons as he tried to remember the last time he'd put it on, worn it to a function. He supposed it had been more than two years before, when he'd gone to a graduation ceremony in Philadelphia. He hadn't actually thought he'd find a brother there, but he would never have known if he had he not worn it. He hadn't found anyone; no one had paused next to him and whispered the sign to him.

The silence in the house became heavy and Lee finally put the pin away and returned the case to the drawer, surprised that his mind had grown quiet enough for him to even notice something so mundane as silence. Still, perhaps that meant that he'd be able to get some work done, despite losing an hour of his evening and having his brains and memories scrambled.

He managed to keep thinking that right up until the moment he turned on the light in his kitchen and saw the table covered with paper, his laptop still open and waiting for him to finish his last sentence.

"Shit." He looked at the mess, the collection of things to read and the notes he had been making up the side of one sheet, the margin turned red with his ink, and knew he probably wasn't going to be able to get back into it that night. All of his energy and drive had drained away, gotten lost in the past that was trying to come back up and occupy his mind.

Not one to give up, however, he did try. The first thing he did was turn around and go back to his bedroom to change out of his good clothes and into worn jeans and a jersey knit top; he even took the time to defiantly mess up his hair even more when he passed the mirror. He didn't need to be neat and tidy in his own home; he was a student. He would study and be comfortable.

However, while he could be messy, his sink could not. Choosing to take yet another few moments before hitting the books, Lee strained the bucket's contents through an old T-shirt and threw the whole mess away in a garbage bag. It was disgusting, but it had to be done, and he wasn't about to dump that slop back down a drain. He'd be the one to get it all back out again, and once was enough. With the bucket rinsed and outside his door so he'd remember to take it up to Joey's in the morning, he steeled himself and headed back to work.

Sitting at the table, his red pen between his teeth like a bit, Lee spent a fruitless twenty minutes trying to get back into his headspace. He read back a few pages, going over the notes he'd made; he scanned through the start of his paper; he even pulled out his notebook and recopied the notes he'd made at his afternoon meeting with his advisor.

When, for the third time, he caught himself staring blankly at the notebook, Lee spit out the pen and rubbed his eyes. He wasn't as keyed up and stunned as he'd been in Joey's apartment, but apparently jumping back into the thick of things was too much to ask.

With a sigh that he felt in his bones, Lee got up and went

to his fridge for a beer, trying to remember where he'd last put his paper address book. He'd moved to keeping phone numbers in his phone and in his computer's address book, but some numbers from the past hadn't been entered; if he didn't call it, he didn't keep it, usually.

Some things never got completely thrown away, however, and move after move, from apartment to apartment, there were bits and pieces that just kept getting packed and taken with, even if they were never touched until the next move. Lee tended to keep his papers down to the bare minimum; in fact, one of the two drawers in his filing cabinet was where he kept his ice skates, since it was empty anyway. The folder of stuff he took with him all the time—transcripts, birth certificate, diplomas and degrees—was at the back of the bottom drawer, and behind that he found the old address book, dog-eared and worn.

Using only the light in the kitchen to see by, Lee went to the tiny living room and sat down, his beer cradled between his thighs as he angled the address book to see the names scrawled on the pages, some in pencil but most in the black roller ball gel ink pens he'd favored at CSUC.

It took him a moment to decide which person to call, flipping back and forth between the people who he knew would really get it. He was vaguely ashamed to realize how much time had slipped away between phone calls and meetings; these were the people he had loved most in his life, other than his parents and grandparents, and he'd gotten too busy to call, too rushed to do more than send the occasional holiday card.

He'd thought one only reached that stage when one was old and settled, not when one was only a few years past graduation. But people moved, a lot, and there was always something to do. Making time for old friends had fallen down the list, and it took a surprise, a need for a certain type of conversation, for him to realize it.

Finally, he admitted that there really was only one first choice for this call, and he reached for the phone. The number beside the name was years old and was likely not even current; it was all he had, though, so he punched in all eleven digits, sat back on the couch, and held onto his beer bottle like it was a lifeline. Matt would forgive him for fading away; he knew it.

The phone rang three times before a male voice answered. "Hello?"

It wasn't Matt, but that wasn't really a surprise; Lee had never known Matt to live alone. He had time for a very fleeting thought about how foolish the assumption was that he even still knew the most basic things about Matt, given the gap between then and the last time they'd talked—and an even more fleeting impression that he was really over thinking things. "Hi," he said, pleased that his voice sounded normal even if his mind was jumping all over the place. He had to clear his throat before he could continue, though, suddenly frantic that he'd lost Matt forever. "I'm looking for Matt Lewis, but I've had this number for a long time and he might have moved. Would he be there?"

"You're in luck, man. The number is right and he's around here somewhere. Hang on." There was a loud sound like something falling over and a muffled curse. "He's out in the garage, I think—can I tell him who's calling?"

Relieved, his heart suddenly pounding hard, Lee licked his lower lip nervously and started nibbling at it. "It's Lee. Thanks."

"No problem." Lee could hear walking, a door opening, a few more steps; finally the voice called out, "Hey, Matt. Phone for you. Guy says his name is Lee."

This time the sound wasn't so much of something falling over but more of metal banging on metal. A voice was lost under the noise, but Lee found himself smiling. He knew exactly what was going on, and he could picture Matt bent over a car engine with such clarity that it was like a sharp stab in his heart that he'd ever forgotten it.

"Uh, he's got his head in his Jeep, man." The guy sounded apologetic. "He says Lee who?"

Lee winced and screwed his eyes shut before capitulating to the inevitable. Damn it. "Tell him it's Scout." God, he'd kill Matt when he got him on the phone.

"Matt! Dude now says his name's Scout!"

"Scout!" Matt yelled the name, drawing out the vowels until the whole thing was about ten seconds long. "Don't you dare let him hang up!"

"Uh, did you hear that?"

Lee snorted a laugh. "Everyone heard that. My neighbors heard that."

"Guess he knows who you are, though. Here you go."

Lee grinned as Matt took the phone, still yelling. "Scout, Scout, Scout! I used to know a guy named Scout but he stopped calling, didn't send any flowers, not even freaking Christmas cards! You wouldn't be that Scout?"

"Nope," Lee said, shaking his head and grinning, his smile so wide it hurt his cheeks. "I'm not that Scout. Must be some other guy."

"Son of a bitch, how many years has it been?" Matt's voice was loud, crowing over the line. "Six?"

"Good God, no. Three, maybe. Hell, we were still tooling around town in your old Civic six years ago, in grad school."

"Bite your tongue." Matt sounded just as insulted as Lee thought he would. "I have never owned anything like a Civic."

"Reliable, hard working, fuel efficient..."

"Did you call me up to insult me?" Matt was laughing, though, just like always. "What's up? Hey, are you in town? God, give me an hour, I'll meet you. Where are we going?"

"Easy, Jem. Chill, I'm not in town. I'm still at Legacy; not done with my doctorate yet."

"Okay, give me six hours and I'll meet you."

Lee took a long swallow from his beer. "You would, wouldn't you? You really would."

"I would." Matt's voice grew serious. "Do you need me to? I'll be there by morning."

"Nah." Lee sighed and drank again. "But thanks."

"What's up? For real." Lee heard a fridge door open and the rattle of glass. He knew the sound of beer bottles.

"I..." Lee suddenly realized he had no idea where to begin. "I'm working on my PhD, right? Remember that tiny-ass place I was living in my first year here?"

"The one that counted a closet as the second bedroom you were planning to use for an office? God, yes. That was my lesson in never having a year long lease, dude."

"Mine, too." It had been even worse than the single room he'd had in the rooming house for the full four years at CSUC. At least then he'd known that he had one room and that things would get better. That first apartment of his own, though, had stung. "Anyway, as soon as that lease was up I got the hell out of there. I rented a loft from a guy who knew a guy and the year after that I moved again. I needed a place for cheap, I needed quiet to study and work on my dissertation, and I needed to not have a roommate for the same reason."

"Uh-huh, with you so far. You got a problem where you're living?" Matt sounded concerned, which wasn't what Lee wanted at all.

"I'm telling this all wrong." Lee sighed and closed his eyes, sinking down on the couch. "Okay, shorter version. Right now, for the last year, I've been living in a gated community. It's condos and townhouses and very nice and pleasant, very upper middle class feel with big money behind it. For the use of a little bungalow off in a corner—which is actually very nice, if insanely small for a house—I'm a sort of groundskeeper slash property manager. I keep the lawns nice, clean the pool, do minor repairs; that sort of thing. I do manual labor for a few hours a week and I get to live my life and I only need to pay for... well, everything but the rent and utilities. I even get free internet and central air. It's a pretty sweet deal."

"Thank God you're a freaking genius. Full ride scholarships, man."

"I never had a full ride, Matt." Lee smiled; it was an old discussion. "I had tuition and books, remember? I still had to wait on tables a million hours a week, and I still had to chase bursaries. Besides, it doesn't really work that way at the doctorate level. I do, however, know how to write a pretty decent grant proposal and I get a stipend or two from the school for some other things. I'm doing okay." He was actually just scraping by, but it was enough to keep him from accruing debilitating debts, as long as he had no actual social life or hobbies that cost money.

"Good for you, Scout. Wring 'em dry, get your degree, keep on truckin'. Am I right or am I right?"

Lee could almost see Matt saluting him with his beer bottle. "You're right. Hey, you learn how to wear your ball cap properly yet?"

"Backward is properly. Don't change the subject."

Lee groaned and pinched the bridge of his nose. "Okay. All right. Here we are." He took a breath and made himself say it, more than sure he was making a far bigger deal out of everything than Matt would. "I found a brother tonight. Here, where I'm living. He's a resident in one of the units. I clean his pool and fix his plumbing."

There was a moment where Lee could predict exactly what curse words were about to pour forth from Matt's end of the line. Happy or angry, Matt was always a fountain of profanity, usually to Lee's amusement. Matt was inventive with his cussing and he had family in the south; sometimes Lee wasn't even sure something was foul until he'd thought about it for a while.

It was a night of surprises, though, the latest one being the long pause followed by a low whistle and Matt saying, "That is so awesome. I can't even begin to tell you how jealous I am."

"You're jealous?" Startled, Lee opened his eyes. "That's your first reaction?"

"Well, sure." Matt laughed at him, his voice warm. "What did you think I'd feel? Worried? He's a brother, Scout. Family. There's no bad there, even if by some bizarre twist of fate you don't get along. That's happened, what, once that we've seen out of how many guys?"

"Um." It was the best he could do. Lee drank his beer and tried to be slightly less flummoxed.

Matt, being Matt, was chuckling again. "We knew almost thirty brothers in our time at CSUC. That's a hell of a big family to be part of, and there was just Phil and Cesar who clashed. Remember the way they used to bitch at each other about every little thing? Oil and water, those two."

Lee nodded. Phil and Cesar had almost come to blows once or twice in the two years that Lee had known them through TCF. "Personality issues."

"Uh-huh. Both of them were awesome guys, but man. And remember what happened when Cesar got ditched by whatsisname? You know, that tall drink of water who thought he had a magic dick. Luis."

"God, I'd forgotten him." The aftermath of the breakup had been painful to watch, so painful that Lee had never let himself wonder what it really and truly felt like for Cesar; living in the halo of his pain was hard enough. "Cesar was gone on him, totally planning a rainbow life with unicorns and bows. He was messed up for a long time after Luis broke up with him."

"Right, and it was Phil of all people who sat him down and said what Cesar needed to hear in words that would get through and stick. I was there, I saw it." Matt made a noise that sounded like admiration. "I thought I was still drunk when the two of them wound up curled up in the easy chair for most of an afternoon while Cesar talked it out with him."

Lee'd been working that day but he'd heard about it at the time. Still, it hadn't made as big an impression on him as it apparently had on Matt. "You still think about that? After all this time?"

"Dude." He could hear Matt's bottle click against Matt's teeth, something he'd forgotten Matt did when he was thinking. "That was the definition of TCF, to me. They fought, they had clear reasons for not getting along, they wouldn't have hung out on their own. But Phil stepped up to take care of his brother and Cesar trusted him enough to let him." The laughter was gone from Matt's voice and he spoke quietly, not rushing his words. "That's what The Chosen Family was all about. The way Ken helped you out, the way Phil helped Cesar. Those promises we made are for life, man. Look at you. Reaching out to me because you're freaked. It's cool, I get it, I welcome it. But, yeah. Jealous that you have a brother close to you."

Lee didn't say anything for a moment, humbled by Matt's tone and his words. He sat in the dark of his living room and drank beer and felt vaguely embarrassed for how he'd reacted to Joey and the pin. Matt always seemed to float through life, happy and content and not flipping out because someone was nice to him. "Joey's happy, too," Lee finally said. "He hugged me, called me brother. Said I'm like him."

"Heh. I like him already. That's cool, man. I'm glad for you—still jealous, though."

"God." Lee sighed, long and loud. "I felt like such a... It wasn't pretty, Matt."

"That's because you have, like, fifty-percent social skills. I love you anyway." Matt snickered at him softly. "Tell me about him, come on."

Lee turned on the couch and pulled his legs up so he could stretch out. "Um, Joey Reed. He's class of '97. Doctor of... uh, some kind of chemistry. He works for a pharmaceutical company, in research and development, I think."

"Young and smart. Cool. What does he look like? Big science geek?"

That made Lee laugh. "Only if big science geeks are the new hot."

"They are, actually."

"Oh. Well, he's old school, then. All square jaw and expensive haircut and gym-toned body. And his shirt was hand-tailored—he was going to some awards thing tonight—and I know that the art on his walls was a mix of high end prints and original paintings. He's every inch the successful career man."

"Why, Scout. You sound like you're plumb impressed." Matt could be a bit of a bastard. "Honestly, try to get an ounce more envy into your voice. Or maybe call someone who doesn't know you as well, next time. You'll get there, you know you will. You'll have fancy clothes and expensive junk around to impress your pool boy."

Lee rolled his eyes and drank from his beer bottle. "I

know. I'm not jealous. Just telling you what I saw."

Matt laughed at him. "I know you," he repeated. "You've been working for what he has since you were born, my friend. Maybe he has, too. Maybe that five years he has on you is all the difference."

"Maybe he had a head start."

"Maybe you should get to know him before you jump to conclusions." The laughter had died out of Matt's voice again. "Give him a chance, Lee. He's a brother, and you can't just go around being snide about everyone who's successful and has a little bit of money. You just can't."

For a fraction of a second Lee considered saying a polite good night and ending the call, but he came to his senses almost immediately. This was why he'd called Matt and not Tony. Tony wouldn't have jumped right into his head and the icky stuff that lived there; Tony was too fond, too proud of Lee to do that. He was blind, whereas Matt was willing to go in and stir up the muck, secure in knowing that Lee would still love him when the world was murky.

"You still there?"

Lee sighed. "Yeah, Jem. I'm here. God damn it."

Matt laughed again, his voice warm. "Lecture over. But I reserve the right to come back to this point at any time in the future, as per our mutually agreed upon promises of not letting you get away with shit."

"I beg your pardon? There was no mutual agreement." Lee would have remembered agreeing to something that absurd, even if they were drunk as frat boys. Which they most definitely were not—that drunk, or even frat boys.

"You agreed to letting me be your conscience by your complicit behavior—i.e., calling me." He sounded very pleased with his logic, even smug.

"Can we move along now?" Lee was certain he was being even more complicit in not putting up a fight, but it didn't really matter; in a sense, Matt was right. When Lee needed his butt kicked, he called Matt. He knew that he'd hear truth, or very close to it.

"Sure. How did you figure out that this paragon of success, this hottie of the sciences, this resident in your own personal Melrose Place is a brother of The Chosen Family?"

"Plumbing issue." Lee filled Matt in, being careful to impart the full horror of Bernie and not to linger on the furniture, decorations or anything else that might show he'd observed the material aspects of Joey's success, and finished up with the obvious pleasure that Joey'd had at finding a member of TCF. "He was really excited," Lee said softly. "Like you would be, I think."

"Like you should be," Matt told him. "Honestly, Scout. The Family is a good thing—it was fantastic for you when we were at CSUC and it can be again. If you and Joey don't mesh or don't become really good friends for whatever reason, that's okay. You'll still know that he's got the basic personality strengths that you admire and that you can trust him. That's not bad. So get over yourself and spend some time with him, okay?"

Lee was glad he was sitting in the dark, and that they were talking over the phone. Having to face such sincerity head on would be trying, and no doubt he'd find himself feeling even more foolish than he already did. "Yes, Matt," he finally said. "I'm not going to push him away, really I'm not. I just... I was surprised, is all. Well, shocked and kinda freaked out." Lonely, and suddenly aware of it. Lee's eyes burned hot.

"I know," Matt said softly. "I do."

"But you think my time to wallow in hating the surprise is up."

"You get an hour per shock, unless it involves babies, marriages or death. Then you can wallow a little longer."

Lee looked at his watch. "Damn it."

"Right on. So, over it?"

"I will be." Lee rolled his eyes. "Thanks, Matt. Who answered the phone, by the way?"

"Ah, finally! Now we can talk about me?"

"Now we can talk about you." Lee got up and went to get another beer from the fridge. "Catch me up, Jem."

Chapter Four
Cloaks and Keys

Lee was so nervous he thought he might be sick. He had no idea what the hell he'd been thinking, agreeing to become part of some weird secret society. He knew exactly what was going to happen. He'd traded a shift at the Stomping Grounds, wound up with three hours less on his schedule, and for what? So he could pace his room and get stood up, leaving him humiliated and poorer than he really could stand, or—worse—he'd be blindfolded and taken to God only knew where to be marched around, stripped naked, covered in sticky stuff and toilet paper and left to find his own way home.

If there were two true things about Lee Sutton, they were that no one could come up with worse scenarios than he could, and no one could upset him as much as he could himself.

He could hear the guys he shared a kitchen with out there, drinking beer and planning their night. Music was thumping his floorboards, the noise level fairly constant from eleven a.m. on Saturdays to about nine p.m. on Sunday, save for a few hours when everyone was passed out. Of course, there were only about three guys in the whole boarding house who were old enough to buy alcohol, but they did it for everyone, every weekend.

The only thing that made the house bearable at all was the rent for his room and the locks on every door and cupboard in the kitchen. No one stole Lee's things. Lee couldn't afford to have anything stolen, and when he couldn't afford to buy beer he could at least lock himself in his room and study when it was too loud to sleep. If he wasn't studying to keep his scholarships, he was working to pay the rent and for food; he didn't cause trouble, he never asked anyone to turn down the volume and he never brought girls around—his housemates all loved him.

As much as he tolerated his housemates in return, Lee didn't want them seeing Tony coming to fetch him and taking him out with a blindfold on. Of course, Lee was reasonably sure that Tony would do no such thing. How could one maintain a secret if one was walking around with blindfolded people? Still. Lee's pacing was kicking up to a frenetic level, and if someone came looking for him it would be best if he at least appeared not to be freaked out, if he couldn't manage to look totally calm.

He could wait for Tony outside on the sidewalk. Sure, it was January and freezing, but it had to be better than the continual loop of steps around his mattress.

And he didn't want Tony to see his room. He didn't want anyone to see his room. Not because of the mess, as there wasn't one, but for the lack of things to make a mess with. He had a mattress and blankets and pillows. A dresser. His books, stacked neatly along the wall, and on his window sill he had a cup full of pens that he picked up and collected when he happened across them at the library or in classes. His bike hung on one wall, waiting for a new tire, the spokes snapped and the wheel bent from some asshole trying to break his lock. At least the bike hadn't been stolen, merely rendered unusable until he could buy a wheel and a new tire.

His room was neat enough, and he had his music and his grandmother's tiny TV, but it sure wasn't the kind of place one invited friends to see. The thought of it, of issuing an invitation to Tony or anyone else, had Lee pulling open his closet and getting his coat and keys.

"See you later," he said, locking his door behind him. His room was right next to the kitchen, and there were four people looking curiously at him.

"Working, man?" Jason was sitting on the counter, his beer bottle held loosely with long, elegant fingers.

"Not tonight, just going out. See you in the morning."

A chorus of words—some wanting to know who he was going out to bang, some yelling out the names of clubs and bars they were going to try to get into—followed him down the stairs and out into the night. Lee didn't reply to any of them; he figured no one would notice anyway and they'd probably forgotten about him as soon as he was out of their direct line of sight.

It was dark out, and frost gleamed on the sidewalk, lit up by the glow of the street lights. He lived in an older neighborhood near campus, and the street was lined with trees and evergreen shrubs, each Edwardian or Victorian era home shrouded in some kind of foliage that afforded privacy to the residents. A lot of the houses were one or two units, but the handful of rooming houses seemed to cause the others to want to grow higher bushes and draw their curtains earlier and earlier. Not that Lee could blame them; when he was finished with school and didn't need to live somewhere cheap, he'd be moving as far away from a campus as he could reasonably get.

Lee walked slowly up the length of the block, standing in place when he saw car headlights or heard someone walking, keeping an eye out for Tony. He hadn't thought to ask if Tony was picking him up in a car or not; he hoped so. His hands were freezing and the idea of walking through the streets being led by his hand, eyes closed, just made him want to—

"Lee?"

"God!" Lee turned, his boot heel crunching on the frosted grass between sidewalk slabs. "You scared the crap out of me."

Tony grinned at him, his hands in the pockets of his red windbreaker. "Nervous?"

Lee didn't see any point in denying it. "Yeah."

"That's cool. Come on, I'm parked around the corner." Tony started walking, back toward Lee's house. "Party at your place this weekend?"

"Every weekend." Lee rolled his eyes and kept pace. "It gets loud. Usually I'm at work, though, or they all take off to a bar or a house party by eleven and I can study for a couple of hours."

Tony glanced at him. "You don't ever just have fun? Get a little drunk with them, take a night off?"

"Couple times, right after mid-terms or finals." Lee's hands were really cold, so he put them in his jeans pockets. "They're not my friends. Just people I live with."

Tony nodded. "I lived on campus for three years. I know what you mean." They rounded the street corner and Tony pulled a set of keys out of his pocket and pointed to a battered looking Saturn at the curb. "Here we go."

Lee's stomach turned to lead as he settled himself into the passenger seat. "Got a good heater?" He hoped he sounded relaxed and calm, even though he had already admitted to nerves. Like every other weekend was spent joining organizations he knew nothing about and taking oaths that he assumed he'd be expected to keep.

For all the absurdity of it, for all his panic and thought-up paranoia in his room, Lee had no doubt that the society existed and that he was joining something real, something that would affect him deeply and in lasting ways.

He also knew that he wanted it so badly he could feel an ache in his bones whenever he let himself dwell on the what-if-Tony-made-it-up. Without more than the barest hint of what it was, Lee already belonged, had already given himself over to this group of men.

Tony started the car and almost immediately warmth flowed from the vents, blasting Lee's legs and chest. "Put this on, please." Tony held out a strip of black cloth. "It's just a scarf. Mine, actually, so it better not snow tonight." His smile was warm and friendly. "It'll be okay, Lee. It's all right to be nervy."

Lee, not trusting himself to speak, nodded and took the scarf. By the time he had it tied over his eyes, well enough that he couldn't see a thing and positioned so Tony wouldn't even suspect him of trying to see anything, the car had pulled away from the curb and they were on their way.

Tony had said that Lee would be told where they were during the ceremony—or at least at some point that evening. Still, he took what Lee assumed to be a very indirect route to where they were going. They turned often, so often that Lee knew they were going in circles, then going to a whole other part of town, then doing more circles. They drove for what felt like an hour but absolutely had to be longer than twenty minutes, even if Lee's perception of time was fuzzy. They crossed railway tracks, went over at least two bridges—or the same one twice—and did a significant stretch of highway driving where they didn't turn at all, let alone stop for a light or stop sign.

Tony said nothing the entire time. He didn't play any music, and he didn't hum. Lee didn't try to engage him, as there seemed to be no point. Lee had no idea what he'd ask, anyway.

Finally, the tires crunched on gravel, the car slowing and turning sharply. "When I stop," Tony said quietly, "stay where you are. I'll come around the car and help you out, lead you in. Okay?"

Lee nodded, not trusting his voice. His mouth had suddenly gone dry. With a cough to clear his throat, he nodded a second time. "Sure."

The car stopped and Lee felt it rock slightly when Tony put it in park, then shut off the engine. A door creaked, the car shifted as Tony got out, and cold blasted in for a moment until the car door slammed. Lee could hear Tony walking, his shoes on gravel mixed in with the sound of the engine ticking as it cooled, then Lee's door opened and the winter air rushed in again.

"Here we go." Tony's hands helped Lee stand and move back a few steps, and the car door closed with a solid thunk. "We're going to go in. There may or may not be voices, depending on who all is here. We'll go into a large entry and I'll have you stand while I change into my... while I change. Then you and I will go in, and we'll wait for the others. After that, just follow along and speak when you're asked questions."

Lee nodded, disoriented and wishing he hadn't just spent ages in a moving car in the dark. "Hang on a moment, okay?"

Tony's hands tightened briefly. "Okay? Feel sick?"

"A little." Lee breathed through his mouth. "The cold is helping."

"Let me know when you're ready."

Lee didn't think he'd ever be what one could call ready, precisely, but he could manage close to it. The ringing in his ears backed off and his circulation approached normal. He heard another car pull up, however, and his heart started to race. "Okay, we can go in now."

Tony laughed softly, like he knew what Lee was thinking. Drawing things out could only make it worse. "Here we go." Tony took Lee's arm as if he were leading a blind man, guiding him but not tugging or pulling. "One small step up here."

Lee stepped, heard a door open and felt a wash of warm air before Tony urged him inside. "Any more steps?"

"Nope." Tony's hands guided him forward and then to the left for a few paces. "Stand here." He let go, and Lee could hear Tony's coat zipper being pulled and fabric rustling. "Hey, man. How many are we waiting for?"

It took Lee a startled moment to realize Tony was talking to someone else. His ears strained to hear how many people might be in the immediate area. Not that it mattered, he reminded himself. He'd find out soon enough.

Lee's palms began to sweat so he jammed his hands into his jeans pockets and tried not to fidget.

A quiet voice replied to Tony. "Two more. Need any help?"

"Nah, I've got it. Thanks, though. We'll be right in."

Footsteps, not loud, moved away from them and cool air slid over Lee's face as the exterior door opened. Lee turned his head that way, once more trying to find any kind of information to incorporate with what he had.

A large entry, hard surface floor, no closet door open and closing, no echoes. Essentially, he had nothing to go on.

Tony's hand—Lee assumed, and how disturbing to think it might be someone else's—touched Lee's shoulder. "I'm going to take your coat off you and hang it up, then we can go in."

Lee nodded and pulled his hands out of his pockets, but Tony was ahead of him, lowering the zipper and sliding Lee's coat off his shoulders. "Okay, that's just weird feeling." Lee let him take the coat, but wished more than ever that he could take off the blindfold. "How much longer?"

"We'll go in now. There's just one person left, I think." Tony's voice was oddly muffled, but he took Lee's arm just as he had a few minutes before and Lee let him. There was something about the steadiness of Tony's arm, the tranquility in his voice that leant Lee a bit of needed calm. If Tony was sure, Lee could be less unsure.

They walked slowly but steadily, the pace even. Lee didn't stumble, willing to let Tony lead; he was too far into the process to balk at walking with help, after all. He had no idea where he was or who was in this place with him; what good would it do to fumble around trying to find his way on his own when he had a guide?

Under his feet, the sounds changed. The hard surface floor remained hard, but it changed. Perhaps from tile to wood, or from vinyl to tile. Lee wasn't sure, he only knew the sounds around him were bigger, deeper. He could hear people moving, a few muffled coughs, fabric shifting. His boots sounded on the floor, not ringing but not muted, either.

He could smell sulfur from matches, and wool. He thought maybe he could smell garlic as well, and tomatoes. Maybe there was food. That would be good. All was not lost when there were snacks to be had.

They stopped walking and Tony turned Lee slightly to face another direction. Forward, backward, Lee had no idea. "Stand here," Tony whispered in Lee's ear, his voice still odd. "We're going to start very soon."

Lee nodded. He stood, not sure what to do with his hands, and listened to the sounds around him. Still gentle movements of cloth, the odd rustle. No one speaking. He could hear another set of footsteps and the rustling increased, grew with an intensity so subtle and sleek that

Lee thought perhaps he'd imagined it and there was no reason for his pulse to be drumming so hard that he was vibrating with it.

"Gentlemen."

Lee jumped and Tony's hands—he hoped, again—settled on his shoulders.

The voice was clear and calm, deeply pitched, and seemed to come from everywhere. It took most of Lee's attention not to turn his head about, trying to locate the speaker.

"Brothers." It was the same voice, but not quite as loud. This time Lee could tell that the speaker was in front of him, and was not, in fact, resounding from all directions. Tony's hands squeezed him in what Lee assumed was supposed to be a reassuring manner.

"A new year has begun and we gather once more. I've missed you."

A low murmur filled the room, almost a buzz as distorted voices replied, so softly that Lee couldn't even make out what Tony said.

"It is time to welcome new brothers. Seniors, are you confident and sure in your choices?"

"Yes." Lee heard Tony that time, and other voices nearby.

"We thank you for finding them for us." There was a pause, another buzzing murmur, and then the lone speaker moved. His steps were firm and measured, and within moments Lee could tell he was walking a slow circle, around at least himself and Tony, perhaps others. "We live in a country where we can expect not to be coerced, and this group values that freedom. You have been brought to us in blindfolds, but they will be removed shortly, we promise. This is not done to keep truth from you, but to maintain your choices. Now that you are here, now that we are gathered, it is up to us to share with you what we are. Only then may you choose what is right for you, and right for us.

"We are family. We will listen to you."

Tony's hands flexed on Lee's shoulders and a chorus of voices said, "We will hear."

"We will talk with you," said the lone voice.

The murmur, hushed and serious, replied, "We will encourage."

"We will protect you."

In unison feet stamped, once. "We will defend."

"We will be your brothers."

Again, feet stamped on the floor, Tony's body rocking Lee's as the voices, louder, declared, "We are The Chosen Family."

In the silence that followed Lee realized he was holding his breath and let it out slowly.

"There are rules." The deep voice was calm. "You may not tell anyone that we exist. You must understand that while the oath of brotherhood is life long, we do not exist in order to ensure your success after graduation—we are here to support and defend and even love you for the next four years. It is our primary goal to be your family at CSUC."

Lee nodded, the movement unconscious until it happened, but by then it had been done and he couldn't undo it.

"There are expectations. You will be expected from tonight onward to be a brother. That means you will help where you can. You will be discreet and not reveal knowledge you gain within these walls to anyone else. That includes the very basis of our bond—you will not out a brother. Some of those here tonight have very valid reasons for not being known as homosexual, and you will respect that. You will help us maintain and care for this building, out of respect for those who came before and for those who will come after."

A whisper started up, behind him. A bare breath, the word hardly loud enough to hear, and then other voices joined in, soft but growing. "Choose. Choose. Choose."

"It is time to choose. If you have decided that we are not what you want, you may go from this place with the one who brought you and we wish you well. There will be no one to stand in your way and we will not speak of this again.

"You have been chosen by our beloved and we know you four to be men of honor. We ask you now for your word. Matthew Evan Lewis, will you join us?"

From Lee's right a voice said, "I will." He sounded like his mouth and throat were as dry as Lee's.

"Nathan Scott McGinn, will you join us?"

Nathan's voice cracked. "Yes."

A hand touched Lee, flat on his chest, over his pounding heart. "Harper Lee Sutton, will you join us?"

Lee nodded. "I will. Yes."

Tony's fingers dug in. "Yes," he hissed in Lee's ear. "Thank you."

Lee almost missed the last name, both from the way blood was roaring in his ears and Tony's voice.

"Barney James Turner, will you join us?"

"Yes. Yes."

Tony pulled the blindfold from Lee's eyes and immediately gripped his shoulders again, forcing Lee to look dead ahead. Lee's first impression was that he was looking at the Emperor from the Star Wars movies. Everyone—almost everyone, he amended at once—was wearing robes with hoods so deep he couldn't see their faces. They were all black, or maybe dark gray, and belted at the waist as if worn by cloistered monks. Directly in front of him stood a guy Lee's own age wearing jeans and a blue striped T-shirt, looking around with huge eyes.

Candlelight. Robes. A flash of white under one of the hoods.

The four of them were in the middle of a circle, looking at each other and blinking as their eyes watered, each with a cloaked man behind them. And two more behind that.

The lone speaker was nowhere to be seen, or at least he wasn't in the middle as Lee had expected a leader to be.

"We are the Brotherhood of Leuce," Tony said. "We are the erastea. You are eromenos. We welcome you."

To Lee's left, the man behind the blinking new brother said, "You will be given a marker to wear later in life. If you ever see one like it, you will show respect, and respect will always be given to you. Know that you are family. You were chosen. You are worthy."

Lee's eyes burned and he blinked rapidly, unwilling to show how deeply hearing the words had struck.

Across from him came, "You will learn the sign and counter sign. You will learn our story. You will learn our history and you will, in time, bring to us new brothers. Because we ask it of you."

On Lee's right the man behind the boy with blond, unruly curls said, "As you promise yourself to us, you will be given these things and more. Our story, our words. A task to fulfill. A signal to wear. A key to this house. A robe, a mask. A family. Are you ready?"

As he said the last word all of the robed men pulled their hoods off and stood with masked faces, white and black and blue, silent and still.

"Are you ready?" he asked again.

Lee nodded and caught sight of the others doing the same. He didn't know about them, but he was fairly sure he couldn't speak. He hoped it wouldn't be required.

"Eromenos, kneel."

They did as they were told, although in Lee's case it was more of a slow folding as he tried to go to his knees without falling over. Once down he realized that the four of them had been placed at the center of a quartered circle, the lines a part of the wooden floor. The circle was inlaid, and in each quarter were four men, three robed and a new brother at the tip.

"Do you swear to keep the secrets of the brotherhood and to keep both your mind and heart open with your chosen family? If so, say 'I do.'"

"I do." All four of them spoke as one.

"Do you swear to use your talents to aid your brothers when asked? If so, say 'I do.'"

"I do."

"And do you swear that you will respect the men in this room and treat them with the kindness they are promising you, putting their needs on par with your own? If so, say 'I do.'"

"I do."

"Seniors. Gift your Juniors."

The rustle of moving fabric grew and Lee leaned back as Tony angled his body over Lee's, placing a bundle on the floor in front of him. They each had one, a neat fold of cloth topped with a small, thin book that looked like it had been printed and bound years ago and three shining objects: a locker key, a house key and a gold, triangular lapel pin. Tony's mask was on Lee's bundle, and a quick look up showed him that the men who had brought the others had also removed theirs. He didn't know any of them.

Lee looked at the bundle but didn't reach for it, waiting for some kind of signal. He looked to his right and found the curly haired guy looking back, giving him a crooked grin. Lee smiled back and nearly jumped out of his skin when the dozen men around them started speaking at once.

"Achilles and Patrocles, Alexander and Hephaestion.
Heroes in life, legends in death.
Bones mixed, one soul in two bodies.
The Brotherhood of Leuce.
Beloved, inspired, cherished and protected.
The Chosen Family.
We are the Brotherhood of Leuce
Grown by four. Welcome, brothers."

Lee and the others looked up, Lee wondering what the hell ancient Greeks had to do with anything at all, and suddenly their new family was hooting and dancing, masks and robes flying off as hands reached to pull Lee and the others to their feet.

Passed from hand to hand, hugged and greeted and kissed on both cheeks, Lee slowly came to realize that it was done. He was a brother and he had family.

A big, noisy family that was ready to party.

Chapter Five
Family Meeting

A week after Lee both retrieved Bernie's diamonds and Joey's pin from the sink and also returned the bucket, he was at his kitchen table with a bowl of stew forgotten and cold beside his notes while he powered through a chapter of his dissertation. He'd completely lost track of time, his hunger, even his physical comfort as night had fallen. By the time he looked up, squinting and wondering why his back was so sore, his eyes were itchy from trying to read by the light of his computer screen.

The chapter, however, was done, and that was all that mattered. A rush of endorphins spilled through his body as he stood up, both from the jolting ache of his muscles and the intense feeling of accomplishment. He'd noticed the same sensation at the end of each chapter; he was almost certain that actually finishing the dissertation was going to feel like sex. Maybe even better, if he was lucky.

His eyes watered when he turned on the overhead light, but in a moment he was able to see well enough to clear off the table. He made it a habit to put everything away at the end of the day because trying to eat his breakfast while facing waiting books was far too much pressure. He liked to at least have a cup of coffee into himself before the weight of chapter deadlines fell upon him.

Lee sometimes wondered what getting a doctorate must be like for people who weren't passionate about their field, if it was even possible to go through the grind and intense focus for something one didn't love. He adored political theory, enjoyed the reading, talking, keeping up with papers and discussions and implementations of programs, yet even so there were days he'd much rather skip out and just float in Meadowlark Court's pool without a political thought in his head.

With the books away, the computer off and cooling, a draft of the chapter safely backed up to his thumb drive, Lee picked up the phone and ordered a pizza. He had no idea what time it was, just that it was dark and the stew was too far gone to even attempt heating up again. Besides, he was three days ahead of himself; he deserved a treat.

With a pepperoni and cheese on its way to him via the fine people at Mama Maria's, Lee took a fast shower and let the hot water soothe his back. He didn't hear his second phone, the one provided by the management company for Meadowlark Court, until he shut off the water. He grabbed a towel and hoped that whoever was calling would leave a voicemail for him instead of overreacting and calling in a professional plumber/electrician/pool cleaner/miracle worker. He tended to get in trouble if pros were called in for easy repairs and basic maintenance.

The phone had stopped ringing by the time he managed to get dry enough to walk to his bedroom without leaving puddles, but it started again when he was dressing. Without looking at the caller ID, Lee answered, his jeans undone and his T-shirt not quite all the way on. "Sutton."

"Did you know that I can see your kitchen window

from the upstairs deck off my bedroom? And that the glow of a computer is barely there but the glow of that hideous light fixture is like a beacon signaling you finally took a break?"

Lee had one heart stopping moment when he wanted nothing more than to hang up the phone. Matt's voice, however, had taken up residence in Lee's mind, and Matt was a mouthy, pushy son of a bitch. So Lee took a breath, made himself smile so it would come through in his voice, and made a conscious effort to tease back. "You're stalking me, you know."

"Nonsense. I was sitting there having a beer and checking in to see when I wouldn't be interrupting." Joey sounded amused.

"Ah, but you are. I was in the shower, if that was you calling two minutes ago." Lee tugged his shirt into place, then wedged the phone between his ear and his shoulder to do up his jeans. His jeans really, really needed to be done up and he needed to gather himself enough to be social. To do his best to welcome a brother and to make Matt's voice shut up.

"It was, actually. I was calling back this time to leave an actual message. I didn't the first time. Are you hungry, by any chance?"

"Starving, but there's a pizza on the way." Lee'd been socialized well enough to know that this was the point in the conversation where it would be appropriate to invite Joey to join him, but he held back a little bit. "Mama Maria's."

"There is none finer. How many?"

"Just the one," Lee said with a grin. He had an idea that Joey wasn't going to let him just slip away. That was okay; if Joey was going to do the hard work, Lee was going to let him.

"Well, that's not enough for both of us. Good thing I

have leftovers in my fridge. See you in five." Joey hung up before Lee could say anything further.

Lee looked around his room and shook his head. "He's a brother, all right. It's all about the food." There were worse things; Lee had spent most of his life focused on where the food was coming from, so he understood the language.

He found a pair of socks and went out to await the arrival of both his supper and Joey. The kitchen was clean enough for company since he'd put his books away, but the living room needed some work. The living room, in Lee's opinion, actually needed to be completely replaced by someone who lived a lifestyle Lee wished to become accustomed to. It needed everything, from more square footage to someone else's furniture, maybe even a television that was bigger than seventeen inches. There wasn't anything he could do about it, though, other than turn on one lamp, make sure that the chair was free of lint and hope that Joey wouldn't notice how mismatched everything was.

Lee had done his best, but there was only so much he could do with one decent couch that was actually bought on heavy discount from the scuffed and banged room, and some neat but old furniture from yard sale finds. It was definitely better than first year college student digs, but light years away from an actual grown up home as Lee envisioned things.

A home like Joey's, to put a fine point on the matter.

Thoroughly depressed and annoyed with himself for either not putting Joey off more firmly or for allowing himself to become obsessive again, Lee went into the kitchen and wiped off the already clean counter and table. He might not have much—and nothing worth showing off—but he would at the very least present a clean place. He was also not unaware of the way his moods were rolling up and down; he hoped that food in his stomach and a stiff drink would put a stop to that particular nonsense.

He wasn't sure if he should keep an eye on the driveway next to the privacy wall, watching for his pizza, or out the kitchen window for Joey. His quiet night of celebrating the end of a chapter was turning into nervous pacing.

Lee had just decided to put the radio on, at least, when Joey got there before he could push the button, Joey's arms laden with clanking, rattling bags. "Hey, I'd knock if I could," he called. "Lee?"

"Coming!" Lee hurried to the door and pulled it open, his eyebrows shooting up. "What's all this? I thought you said you were bringing leftovers. Food doesn't usually go 'clink.'"

"That's the bonus, and I did bring food. One of these bags has Chinese." Joey was weighted down, all the clanking bags pulling at his fingers and making his shoulders roll forward. "Can I put these down? Please?"

Lee backed up enough to let him in and tried to figure out how to take one or two of the bags without making him drop the rest. "Put it all on the table, I guess."

"Got it." Joey heaved the bags up and set them down fairly carefully. "Thanks. Is the pizza here yet?"

Lee gave the door a shove. "No, not yet. Their delivery guys don't have wings, so it'll be another few minutes."

"Cool." Joey didn't even look up, just started unpacking one of the bags. "Damn, the shrimp got smushed. Have you got a cloth?"

"Sure." Lee went to the sink and handed Joey the wash cloth, glad that it was fresh and clean, then started to unpack the other bags while Joey mopped up his spill. "Good Lord. When you rob a liquor store you're supposed to take the money, not the booze." He lined up bottle after bottle across the table. "Are you planning to die of alcohol poisoning?"

"I didn't know what you liked to drink." Joey shrugged and started eating shrimp with his fingers from a ripped cardboard box. "So I brought what I had on hand. Well, no. There's probably another fifty bottles of wine up at my place. Next time, we should hang out up there, if you're into wine. Or I can get a little red wagon, I suppose."

Lee knew which option he would prefer but let the topic slide. "There's forks in that drawer," he said, pointing. "You do realize that you're going to have to carry all this back up to your place. Probably drunk, which could get a little tricky." Or even a lot tricky. Next to the bottles of white and red wine there was a collection of booze that would rival any home bar. A six pack of domestic beer, four large bottles of imported—a bitter, a lager, a honey and a red—a bottle of top shelf whiskey, a very good vodka, and half-empty bottle of port. "Port. Interesting choice."

"I thought maybe there was a chance you were insane. I've been trying to get rid of that thing for about two years now."

"It's the only one that's half gone," Lee pointed out as he opened the cutlery drawer and handed Joey a fork, since he hadn't made any move to get one himself. "You drink more port than single malt?"

"No." Joey thanked him for the fork, licked off his fingers and stabbed a shrimp. "I drink a great deal more single malt than port. Thus, a new bottle was needed. Anyway, help yourself to any of it, whatever you like. Oh, and there's some noodle dishes to go with the shrimp and at least half a dozen chicken balls in there, too." He looked vaguely embarrassed. "I was really, really hungry last night when I ordered."

Lee hadn't had free food brought to him in a long time; he hadn't needed it in even longer. Still, it was there and he was hungry, so he started rummaging. Practicality had its place more than pride did. "Thanks. I might even help you carry the booze back up, later." He found the noodles and the chicken balls. "Sit, please." Hooking a chair with his foot, he pulled it around and sat down himself. "I'll wait to get some food into me before I start drinking your bonus gift, though. It'll work out better for everyone, trust me."

"Remember the days when we could drink and eat and stay up late and still make it to a ten a.m. class?" Joey sat down as well and pulled one of the imports to him. "I found out that I couldn't do that any more when I was about, oh, twenty-six." He ate another shrimp, looking totally at ease in Lee's kitchen, like he frequently stopped in for a beer and some takeout. He even slouched in the chair, his hundred dollar jeans stretching tight over one thigh as he rested his foot on the rung of Lee's chair. "I hadn't had anything to drink at all in months; I'd been totally ramped about work. The new guy, you know? Go in early, work late, drag my butt home. Then I had a birthday and the guys said 'hey, man, tie one on!' First time I'd been out drinking since school."

"Peer pressure will kill you," Lee said gravely. The noodles were pretty damn good. There were cashews in there.

"It just about did, I swear to God. I'd never in my entire life had a hangover like that. I think it took me about four days to feel normal again. Then the pictures started turning up in my e-mail."

Lee grinned. "Sucker."

"No photos of that, but there were stories," Joey said blandly as he put the container on the table. "Got a bottle opener?" He held the bottle by the neck.

"Magnet on the fridge." Lee kept picking at the noodles, making a conscious choice to ignore the sucking comment. It was the kind of thing the brothers had said all the time, back when they were studying together, sharing takeout and just hanging out. "So. It's been... what? A week since the big reveal in your bathroom? And you just happen to call me ten minutes after I knock off for the night and finish my work week. Either you're gifted or you really were spying on me from your deck."

Joey opened the beer—the honey—and sat back down, the bottle opener on the table in front of him. He didn't ask for a glass. "Spying is such an ugly word."

"True. What would you prefer?" Lee glanced at the clock, glowing from the microwave. The pizza should arrive any moment.

"How does 'assessing and giving space' sound?" Joey looked thoughtful as he said it, like he wasn't precisely sure himself how it sounded.

"Like you got advice." Lee got up and went to the sink. If he leaned just right he'd be able to see the driveway and spot headlights. "I admit I made a phone call myself."

"Oh, good." Joey laughed and Lee turned his head to look at him. "I'd hoped you say that. So, who did you call? Your Senior, your Junior or one of the guys in your year? I had to flip a coin."

Lee smiled ruefully to himself, remembering the way he'd paged back and forth through his address book. "Did it land right?" Coins very rarely did for him; he'd taken to doing the direct opposite of what any coin toss told him and things had been much smoother for him. It was how he'd picked a graduate school, actually.

"I'm still not sure." Joey grinned at him. "So? Who?"

"Matt." Lee looked out the window again. "He was in my year—my best friend ever, I think. We'd been out of touch, though, and I had to dig around here to find his number. Who did you call?"

"My Senior. I got a lecture."

"So did I."

"Yeah?" Joey sounded amused and Lee turned again to look at him, sprawling even more in the kitchen chair. "I thought only the erastae were allowed to give lectures."

"You've never met Matt, and he is, technically, one of the erastae. Just not to me." A knock at the door had Lee standing even as he added, "We all are, and I seriously can't believe you just used that word."

Joey grinned and saluted him with the beer bottle. "I know them all, man. Erastes, eromenos, Leuce."

Lee paid for the pizza and tipped the delivery guy well; Mama Maria's was the very best pizza around it wouldn't do to have reluctant drivers. "Dig in, Mr. Greek," Lee said as he slid the red and white box onto the table. "Then you can tell me why you keep the old names when we've gone almost completely over to the more accurate terms outside of the Brotherhood ceremony."

"Traditions are very important," Joey said firmly. He opened the pizza box and waited until Lee had passed him a plate before continuing. "Also, the founders named us 'Leuce' for a reason, and not 'The Chosen Family.'"

"Well, sure." Lee slid a slice of pizza onto his plate and licked his fingers. He'd find paper towel later, right then he was too hungry to just stop again. "But you have to admit, TCF is a way better name than some island that's not even called that anymore. Besides, no one knows what it means. The founders were deliberately obtuse."

"Obfuscation with a point," Joey corrected. "They had their reasons and we were all told about them when we were initiated."

Lee snorted and took a huge bite of his too-hot-pizza, chewing and swallowing quickly before he replied. "I had that conversation with my Senior the day he invited me to join. He said that they were too clever—or rather, they were very clever and also tried to appear clever.

They made up the name while chattering over an illegal underaged beer, as a bit of a laugh. The founders, bless them, were prone to drama."

"Sure." Joey nodded and spoke around a mouthful of pepperoni and cheese. "But the whole point of their society—well, not the point, more one of the basic tenets—was secrecy. They gave it an obscure name that does have a meaning to us, the members, and the selection process is dictated by mores that are consistent with the terms erastes and eromenos. Senior and Junior are, I admit, much more wieldy to use, however."

"Erastes and eromenos imply a sexual relationship," Lee argued. "Actually, the words pretty much say it, flat out. I didn't have sex with my Senior, and definitely not with my Junior, as cute as he was." Lee finished his first slice and reached for a second.

"Okay." Joey nodded and didn't say anything at all about his own relationships. "But you have to admit to a level of affection for them both, and there was absolutely the mentoring role, going both ways."

"Of course." Lee chewed his second slice almost as quickly as the first, the cheese still slightly too hot to bear. At least this time he could taste the sauce. "I still maintain that the terms are inaccurate."

"They are." Joey grinned at him and licked sauce off his thumb. "But they sound cool, they're part of our history, and I like to throw them in for the same reason the founders used them: only a member knows what I mean, and... they sound cool."

Lee rolled his eyes and went for his third piece of pizza, finally slowing down. He thought he might even have enough food in his stomach to start drinking beer. "Okay, it sounds all mysterious, I suppose." He got up to grab the paper towels and came back to the table, still thinking about it.

Joey put down his fork and leaned back, his legs stretched out in front of him. "So. We've skirted around the good stuff for a while, you've eaten, we've got booze. Ready to share?"

Lee's eyebrows shot up. "Do you always plan your conversations? Is there an agenda I should see?"

"We're doing okay," Joey told him, grinning. "I have that advice I mentioned, you know. The only thing that kept me from arriving on your doorstep at seven in the morning after that banquet thing was that Ira would have had my balls."

"Ira was your Senior?" Lee looked around and decided the food could stay where it was; there wasn't much left, and he was pretty sure that if it was out the two of them would finish eating it between drinks. "We're getting drunk, right?"

"Only way to have a reunion of this sort. My stomach is too knotted up not to lube the conversation with my bonus gifts." Joey made the confession quickly, and Lee suddenly felt better for it. "And yes, Ira was my Senior." Joey drank from his bottle and pinned Lee in place with a look. "I would have known your Senior, and you'd know my Junior. So? Who brought you in?"

"Tony Sanchez."

Joey's face lit up. "Tony! God, he was fantastic. Always, always feeding people."

Lee snorted. "Sometimes I thought maybe that was his primary motive for inviting me—that and it gave him a great way to gift me with nearly new clothes all the time. It took me a couple of months to figure out I was suddenly dressing better, thanks to him. Tony was—is—a great guy. He's living in Richmond now, doing some kind of finance work. Still with Pete, too. Must be, what, ten years now? Maybe more."

"That's awesome." Joey was still grinning happily.

"God, who else was in his year? Uh, Carmen, I remember the night they were initiated. I thought Carmen was going to puke, and Tony took his new role very, very seriously. Babysat him for about an hour. It was kind of adorable."

"I think Carmen had a thing for Tony, actually."

"Wouldn't be a shock." Joey drank, draining his bottle. "Come on, who else would have overlapped. Echo, of course. He was my Junior."

"It took me months to figure out that that was his real name!" Echo had been a tiny little dude, only a few inches over five feet tall, but he had a voice that sounded like it came from the bottom of a well. Deep and smooth and sonorous, Lee had been sure it had earned Echo a nickname. Instead, it had been a coincidence and all Echo really had were parents with a propensity for strange names. Echo had a brother named Create.

Joey laughed and nodded. "He's a hell of a guy. He's in theater now, working off Broadway."

"Of course." Lee picked up his bottle of beer and then the remainder of the imports with his other hand. "Come on, let's go sit in the living room. It's not a lot more comfortable, but we can put our feet up. Echo was the voice at my initiation."

"Oh, perfect!" Joey grabbed the case of domestic beer and his own bottle, following Lee. "I'm sorry I missed that, really. He would have been awesome."

"He took over the room, man."

"I bet." Joey sat where Lee pointed him, in the good chair, and the two of them settled down to drink. "Crap, we need potato chips."

Lee laughed and took a couple deep pulls from his bottle. "You just ate all kinds of leftovers and even some of my pizza. We'll get chips later."

"Okay. As long as it happens." Joey wiggled in the

chair, his cheeks looking a little pink. "Who else? Um, you would have known Ken Hays, right?"

"Yup." Lee nodded and put his feet up on his coffee table. "He pulled me through my first stats class. We must have sat for seven hours one day while he helped me wrap my head around it." Ken had pulled Lee through something far worse than a stats class, but dark memories could wait before they were shared.

"He designed the Monteith Building, you know." Joey looked incredibly proud of his brother. "And the new wing at the Kerr Facility."

"He's done really well," Lee agreed. "It's not often that architects make the mainstream news, but there he is. People would never guess that he dressed as Carmen Miranda four Halloweens in a row, huh? Nicest legs in his year."

"Oh, God." Joey leaned forward to put his empty bottle on the coffee table and grab a fresh one. "Did you ever see photos of the year Eric, Tony, Dale and Reo dressed as Charlie's Angels?"

Lee laughed, relaxing and letting go of the last of the tension he'd been holding in his gut. They shared a history, Joey and he, and for the first time since he'd left CSUC he could talk about the very best years of his life. "Of course. Did you ever hear about the time Echo's Junior, Charlie, got locked in his storage closet with Matt and Ken? I thought Echo was going to have an aneurysm when we finally got them out. Ken was so embarrassed I thought he'd never stop glowing, and Echo knew it was all Charlie's idea."

"Hey, did you know Charlie followed him to New York?"

"No!"

"True." Joey beamed at him. "I think they have a place in SoHo. I'll call soon, I guess. I want someone, family, to know I found you. More than just Ira, who was deeply concerned that I'd freak you out."

Lee drank the last of his beer and asked, "Why?" He hoped he wasn't the talk of the Seniors. His neuroses weren't that big a deal.

"He knows me, man. He knows I get a little overeager."

"There's nothing wrong with that." Lee got another beer and read the label. "Although you can tell him he was right—I needed some space. I love being a brother, I do. Don't ever doubt that. But me and surprises aren't really good things."

Joey smiled at him. "I'll remember that." He held up his bottle and Lee leaned over to join in a toast, their bottles clinking together. "To brothers, no surprises, and new friends."

Lee nodded. "The Brotherhood of Leuce. The Chosen Family. Right here in Meadowlark Court."

Chapter Six
Elephants on Parade

They traded stories for a while, long enough that the imported beer was long gone and most of the domestic, and Lee finally couldn't take it any more. "Sorry," he said, clumsily getting to his feet, listing distinctly to one side. "I just can't drink that stuff."

"What's wrong with it?" Joey peered into his bottle, one eye screwed shut as he tried to find some lost insight within the brown glass. "It hasn't gone skunky."

"No." Lee had to nod an agreement to that, but he also had to concentrate to stop nodding. "It's okay for what it is. It's just... what it is." Cheap domestic beer that wasn't what Lee liked to drink if there was another choice. "It's a taste I've chosen not to acquire."

"Oh." Joey blinked up at him and seemed to understand. "Well, there's lots of other stuff to drink. What should we have?" He pushed himself out of the chair—twice—and the two of them stumbled into the kitchen. "If you have cranberry juice I can mix up some poor man's Cosmos." He held up the vodka and waved it around. "I think I'm drunk."

"Yup." Lee decided he didn't want a poor man's

anything, thank you very much, and went to the coffee maker. He made sure the basket was empty before he put in a new filter and started counting out scoops of coffee. "Change of plan. First we get a little less drunk, then maybe later we can have some wine or that scotch."

"Okay!" Joey leaned on the counter next to him and watched the precise brewing of coffee. "You're real smart."

"So are you!" Lee grinned, loose and loopy. "You're a doctor."

"But not medical." Joey waved a finger at him. "Chemistry. Not medicine."

"I know." Lee put a hand on Joey's arm, hoping to convey sincerity. "I know. You're a brilliant chemist. No dealing with snotty noses or broken legs for you! Oh, no. You're too smart for that."

Joey beamed. "Right! Too smart to be a doctor." He gripped Lee's arm in return. "And you are a brilliant thinker, going to help the whole world!"

Lee blinked. "Well. I don't know about that. But I do know some stuff about politics and governments and how the world isn't working. And I know enough about me to know that sticking to systems, theory, and conceptual constructs is way better than dealing with people."

For a long moment Joey looked at him earnestly and then he nodded. "That," he proclaimed. "Exactly that. Genius."

Lee laughed and let him go. "I like you," he said, filling the carafe with fresh water. "We need another drink."

"We need coffee!" Joey held onto the cupboard. "And showers and food and then another drink."

"We need showers?" Lee put the water in the coffee maker and started it up, then dug around for fresh forks. "Why?"

Joey took a fork and headed to the leftover food.

"Because showers are a way to sober up. Plus, they make you smell nice."

"I already smell nice. I had a shower earlier."

"You do smell nice." Joey leaned in really close and sniffed him, nuzzling at Lee's neck until Lee got goose bumps. Then Joey nodded and ate a piece of pizza with one hand, holding the fork in the other and gesturing with it. "Do you know what I liked best about our house?"

Lee dragged his mind back from the nuzzle-induced haze and thought. "The pool table? The storage lockers?" Lee had loved those lockers; living in the rooming house for four years meant he used his locker for just about anything he really didn't want to lose. "Oh, I know! The couches and chairs and closet full of spare pillows." He'd also slept there once or twice.

"Uh, I forget. I loved all that stuff. And the big glass windows, even in winter when it was kind of cold. But we didn't have a pool."

Lee nodded. "True. We didn't have a pool; that was out of bounds. But we have a pool now! You and me, right out there. I know, 'cause I take good care of it." He nodded again for emphasis and wished Joey would sniff him again.

"You do!" Honestly, Joey was perhaps the most enthusiastic person Lee had ever met. "I know 'cause I watch you do it."

Lee laughed and ate the Chinese food he didn't remember picking up. "You do?"

"Uh-huh. We all do. Me, Stephanie, Mrs. Clark. Even that guy in the end unit, what's his name? Wetherly?"

"Waverly. And he does not; he's making sure I don't steal anything. Why do you watch me? Do you watch me mow the lawn, too?"

"Uh-huh." Joey grinned at him. "And we watch 'cause you're hot, duh."

Lee rolled his eyes. "Nice. Watch me get all sweaty and gross. You know I'm totally thinking about my dissertation when I'm doing that stuff, right, not getting all sexy?"

"We don't care." Joey opened some cupboards until he found the mugs. "At least, I don't. Steph doesn't, I asked her."

"What?" Lee laughed and shook his head. "You so didn't. She's a nice married lady."

"And we can see each other just fine from our balconies. I watch, she watches, we watch each other watching. It's a whole neighborhood watch situation." Joey drew a sketched out U on the countertop with his finger. "This is my place," he said, putting down a mug. "And this is hers." Another mug was put down to represent the second corner unit. "The... uh, this plate is the pool!"

Lee watched, not pausing as he forked the last of the cashew chicken into his mouth. "Uh-huh. Do we have grass? I ate all the noodles. They would've made awesome grass."

A tea towel around the plate served as grass and Joey stepped back. "There. So you're out there, cleaning the pool or mowing the lawn, right? And I'm on my porch, reading a scholarly journal and making up brand new chemical compositions, as I'm wont to do in my free time."

Lee snorted.

"And Stephanie is over there on her balcony, reading a novel or making up lesson plans, or on her laptop or something. Although probably not the laptop, now that I think about it, 'cause those screens are hard to see in the sun and they get hot on your legs, you ever notice?"

"I've noticed, yes." Lee nodded, wondering when they were going to get to the talking part. "You guys have walkie-talkies or something? Use semaphore? Smoke signals?"

Joey rolled his eyes. "No, no, no. I watch you, right, and then you turn the corner or something and there's a chance you could look up, oh my God! Hey, did you ever notice that you never look up?"

"Why would I look up? I'm tending to the grass and I didn't know I was getting spied on. You better believe I'm gonna look up now, though."

"Look at Steph, not me."

"Why?"

"Because I don't think she cares if you catch her." Joey grinned at him. "I look away when you're facing my place, just in case you look up. And I look waaay over at her place and there she is, watching you. But then she looks at me and we both go 'Whoa.'" He waved a hand in front of his face, like he was fanning off a heat wave. "And then we laugh and go back to watching you." He finished with a flourish and a leer, then picked up the mug that represented his home and filled it with coffee. "Milk?"

"Uh, in the fridge. Do you care if I catch you looking at me?"

"Not anymore." Joey poured milk in the coffee and set the mug aside, then filled up the mug that was representing Stephanie's. "How do you take it?"

"Black, thanks." Lee reached for the mug. "Because we're brothers?"

"Because now I know for sure you're gay and a good person and I can look without worrying that you'll get offended. You won't, right? Get offended?" He looked anxiously at Lee.

"I won't get offended." Lee rolled his eyes and drank the coffee. "You brought me booze and food. I think that earns you at least three free looks."

"Damn, I think I owe you already."

"I haven't started counting yet."

Joey laughed and blew on his mug. "We should go swimming. I can really look then."

"What, now?" Lee looked out the kitchen window. "It's dark."

"The pool has lights!" Joey put his mug down carefully. "Oh, man. We totally should! I bet it would sober us up, too, and then we could drink more!"

Lee tried to find the flaw in the plan, reasonably sure there was one. "What if we're too drunk to swim?" He put his mug down, too, though. A swim at night sounded awesome, and Joey could look and Lee could look and they could get sober and then drunk again. It was perfect, except for the drowning part.

"We need a life guard." Joey nodded and frowned, a crease forming between his eyes. "Oh! I know! We can call Stephanie to watch both of us!"

"What if her husband is home?"

"He can watch, too; I don't mind. He's a fireman, you know. I bet he could save us if we need him to, too, and Steph is pretty small. She'd probably prefer he did it, actually."

Lee nodded. "Okay, perfect. Let's go." He turned on his heel and headed down the hall to his bathroom.

"Where are you going?"

"To get towels!"

"Oh, okay. I'll get ready."

"Good idea." Lee wove his way down the hall, pleased that he didn't need to bounce from wall to wall to stand up, until he got to the linen closet. "Wait, what? Get ready?" He grabbed two towels and ran back up the hall. "What do you mean, get ready?"

"Duh, what do you think?" Joey's shirt was off, draped over a chair, and his shoes and socks were under the table. One hand rested on his fly, the top button on his jeans undone.

"Oh. That." Lee stared. "Nice." Very, very nice. Who knew that chemists had such hard abs?

"Got towels?" Joey was grinning at him, his face flushed with drink and laughing, and he was holding onto the counter with one hand, trying to undo his jeans with the other. "Come on, we'll run up real fast and yell real loud for Stephanie to be our life guard."

Lee saw him start to slide, dropped the towels and made a dash to keep Joey from falling on his ass. Of course, drunk as he was, Lee tripped on the edge of a chair and didn't so much save Joey and provide a nice soft place for him to land.

"Whoops!" Joey started to laugh, and Lee tried to get out from under him, but he was laughing too, which made it difficult. "Are you all right, Lee?"

"I think so." He laughed at the ceiling and took stock. "I banged my elbow, but I think it's okay. I can breathe, and nothing's broken. You?"

Joey hiccupped. "I'm good. What the hell were you doing?"

"You were falling. I was swooping in to save you."

"I swooped once!" Joey rolled over, still giggling, and draped himself over Lee's abdomen. "I swooped from a balcony in my third year—I was helping to do the lighting for a party at one of the social clubs, I think for the Spring Fling. And they were gonna have this girl fly in, you know how Peter Pan and Wendy fly? On wires?"

Lee nodded, his head on the floor, and watched Joey tell the story. He was showing with his hands all the swoops and swirls the unknown girl would take, and Lee was getting dizzy. He followed along anyway, though, soaking up the heat from Joey's body, watching Joey's nipples tighten. Resisted the urge to lick them.

"So there I was, swinging back and forth—" Joey showed him that, too, and Lee realized he'd missed a chunk out of the middle of the story. "I was there for, like, ten minutes until they figured out how to get me down." He grinned and sprawled some more. "When was the last time you took a night off to have fun, Lee?"

"I'm doing it now."

"Before now."

"Can't remember. Doesn't matter." Lee wished Joey would change the subject. He could take time off after his dissertation was done; it would take a few months for his committee to get together for his defense, anyway. He'd get another job to fill in some time, keep researching, interview for jobs—

"Let's go swim." Joey's fingers tugged at Lee's T-shirt. "We should skip calling Steph and just go skinny dipping. She doesn't need to see that—her husband is kind of big and tall. Okay?"

"Okay." Lee said it without thinking, and when something inside him, somewhere at the back of his brain, pointed out that he was about to get himself in trouble, he immediately told it to get another drink and leave him alone. It was probably Matt, anyway.

Joey might have been thinking the same thing, or he thought Lee was kidding. "I mean it," he said with a laugh.

"Me, too." Lee nodded as his sense of right and wrong gave him up for a lost cause and left as ordered. "Come on. Naked." He let Joey pull the T-shirt up and reached down to Joey's fly, his hand yanking down the zipper.

Joey looked for a moment like he was about to start having second thoughts, but then he nodded, too, and wiggled. Lee assumed Joey's sense of propriety had been told off like his own.

"I'm not sure we're gonna go swimming anymore," Joey said, looking down at where Lee's hand was working its way into Joey's jeans.

"Sure we are." Lee's fingers brushed against the soft skin of Joey's belly and he looked into Joey's eyes. "But maybe not right now."

"We're really drunk," Joey whispered. Then he kissed Lee's mouth, sloppy and wet, and Lee had to agree. They were really drunk. It didn't seem to matter very much.

Lee's hand moved, and he wouldn't have been able to say if he intended it or not. Perhaps, like being drunk, it wouldn't have mattered in the long run. All that mattered in that sharp moment was that Lee's fingers curled around Joey's cock and started stroking and that Joey gasped into Lee's mouth and moaned. After that, time seemed to speed up.

They were moving, fumbling with clothes, stripping each other and touching, words stacking and sliding together like a game of Jenga before the blocks were pulled out. Lee couldn't make a lot of sense out of the words, but he really didn't care; he understood Joey's mouth and hands just fine, and the hard length of Joey's erection in Lee's hand spoke volumes. He hated to let it go, and every time he did, so another piece of clothing could be tossed aside, he hurried to reclaim his position.

Joey's mouth tasted like beer and takeout, like college and long nights studying while sprawled on couches. He didn't taste like success or brilliance or even chemistry, although Lee suspected Joey of doing a lot more spying than he had admitted to. Maybe a background check or something. Joey absolutely knew what hot buttons to push. And lick. And even bite.

"God." Lee stared up at the ceiling and blinked slowly while Joey crawled on top of him and went back to mauling Lee's neck, just above the collar bone. "That. Do that. A lot."

Joey laughed, but he bit and licked and his hips were rocking sweetly, pushing his cock through Lee's fingers.

"I got that the first time you said it."

"I said it before?" Lee angled his head a little more to give him room and brushed his thumb over the head of Joey's prick, smoothing fluid. "I really am drunk, I guess. Probably too drunk to get off."

Joey's reply was a shudder and a flex, his pulse thumping against Lee's palm. "Want me to stop?"

"No. No, I didn't say that." Lee's eyes drifted closed and he bent his legs, getting his feet planted for better leverage. "Kiss me."

Joey kissed him and they were getting better at it, far less sloppy and a lot more frantic. Joey's thrusts were getting faster and Lee's hand was getting slick, probably not slick enough to adequately lube the humping, but definitely sticky. He pulled a few more moans out of Joey, too, and when he felt Joey's legs start to shake, Lee lifted his head and looked down to watch.

"Almost," Joey whispered, his lips moving against Lee's neck, wet and slick. "So close. Too drunk, you're right."

Lee shook his head and whispered back. "Look at you." He stroked again, his hand tight. "Look. Watch."

Joey panted and looked, his breath sounding like it was being dragged out of his lungs. "Oh, God."

Lee nodded. "Uh-huh. So hot." He was staring, unblinking, as Joey's cock was swallowed up by Lee's fingers, then pushed through again, hard and burnished and shining. "You, in my hand. Sexy as hell."

Ribbons of come coated Lee's fingers, his belly, and one long strand fell over his own erection, warm and milky. "Lee." Joey grunted, his whole body tight and tense in Lee's arms, and he jerked once more, a weaker pulse pushing out the last of his orgasm.

Lee petted him, smoothed come over them both, grinning. "Better than a swim."

Joey laughed weakly and nodded. "God. When I'm not feeling like I've been hit by a truck I'll return the favor. Gimme two minutes."

"Don't worry about it." Lee would get his, he knew. If not there on the kitchen floor, maybe in the shower. Maybe in bed. Maybe after Joey went back to his condo up the hill and Lee was in bed, remembering. He had no idea when, but he knew he'd get off, sometime. For right then, he could kiss Joey and wait until they were both breathing better.

It only took a few moments; it turned out that the kitchen floor was a horrible place for afterglow.

"Are you ready to go swimming?" Lee asked as Joey climbed off him.

"Are you kidding? I've met the guy who keeps the pool clean. We go in there covered in jizz and he'll be pissed." He laughed and offered Lee a hand up. "Shower first. Then a swim. How does that sound?"

"Like you're getting sober." Lee let Joey pull him up and did his best not to trip on a stray shoe.

"A bit, maybe. That means I probably won't drown in the shower when I go down on you."

Lee grabbed the nearest bottle and drank. He was standing naked in his kitchen, surrounded by booze and clothes, sticky with come, and a guy he barely knew was going to give him a blow job in the shower. It wasn't exactly the life he'd been living in recent years. Or ever, really. "Okay. Ready."

Joey took the bottle and drank, too, then put it down on the table with a clunk. "Ready," he declared. "Where's your shower?"

Lee led the way, pretty much pulling Joey with him, down the hall, into the bathroom with its horrible fluorescent light. The water was cold and it almost killed his wood, but Joey didn't seem to care. He made Lee turn the hot up a little and then went right to his knees, swallowing Joey's cock so fast that they almost fell over.

"Jesus." Lee grabbed the wall with one hand and Joey's head with the other. He wasn't sure if he wanted to pull Joey off him to make sure he was okay, or ram his cock in farther. Maybe he wasn't too drunk to get off, after all.

Joey looked up at him, his eyes wide and his mouth full, water beading in his hair where Lee's body blocked the spray. He winked slowly and sucked quickly, which settled the matter for Lee. Joey's mouth was hotter than the water sliding down Lee's back, and Lee plunged in, encouraged by Joey's look and the hand that was creeping around to Lee's ass, squeezing and kneading.

"Careful," Lee managed to say. "I don't want to choke you." It was true, although it occurred to Lee that he was both too drunk to be really careful and all too happy to pull Joey closer, to get in deeper.

The hand on Lee's ass moved to his balls and Joey pulled off Lee's cock with a pop and a wide grin. "You won't choke me. I've got your balls."

"Good point." Lee nodded, watching his cock bump on Joey's chin then slide along his cheek. "God, you're pretty. Suck me?"

"Spread your legs a bit. Better balance. Is the water heating up?" Joey licked a long swath up Lee's cock.

"Uh. Yeah. Sure." Lee nodded. He wasn't freezing, so the water was warming up. Joey's tongue was pink, flicking out and teasing. "Suck it."

Joey laughed and pushed at Lee's knee, made him widen his stance. "I will. I want to. I've wanted to for a while."

Lee's feet spread and he gripped his cock at the base, guiding it into Joey's mouth. "We'll talk about that later." He moaned when Joey nodded, his balls tingling when Joey started licking and sucking, his head bobbing as he took Lee in deeper and deeper.

Joey sucked cock like he loved it more than anything, ever. He was quick and wet, and he used his tongue, pushing and licking all up and down the shaft. When he let Lee thrust, he didn't stop Lee from going deep, and he wasn't shy about coming off all the way to work his jaw and pay attention to Lee's balls.

That was what did it, in the end. Lee was in a haze, starting to worry that he was going to get blue balls after all, but when Joey mouthed his sac and stroked Lee's dick, the tremors started up. "Oh, fuck," Lee whispered. His fingers tried to dig into the wall. Joey moaned and opened wide to suck on Lee's balls, his hands playing with Lee's dick faster and tighter until Lee went up in his toes and shot, crying out sharply.

He was still shaking when he realized he was kneeling on the bottom of the tub, holding onto Joey and laughing softly. "God, that was... I can't remember the last time I had sex like that."

"In the shower?"

"Drunk off my ass." Lee grinned, feeling loose and easy and pleasantly hammered. "We need to make a promise. Right here and now. Before the water goes cold again."

"Okay." Joey grinned back and kissed him. "What are we promising?"

"No freaking out in the morning. We can talk about it and be all embarrassed if that's the way we wake up, but no freakouts. Okay?"

Joey laughed, louder and more emphatically. "Okay. Deal. Are you prone to freakouts about sex?"

"God, yes." Lee rolled his eyes. "Well, no. I'm prone to freakouts about getting drunk and having sex with someone for the first time while drunk."

"Oh, it's a specific freakout." Joey looked amused, his

cheeks still flushed and his lips swollen from sucking Lee's cock. "As long as you're aware. Would you like to have dinner with me tomorrow? Like, a date?"

Lee blinked at him, then told himself it was merely because there was water in his eye. "A date."

"Yeah, it's when two people go out somewhere together to get to know each other a little, have a good time, be entertained. Sometimes there's food, sometimes drinks, but we might want to pass on that. A movie or a play? Dinner?"

"Um." Lee tried to remember what he had to do for his dissertation, but he'd just finished a chapter and he was ahead of schedule. "Sure? Yeah, I guess. We can go out for dinner, if you want."

Joey nodded. "I want." He kissed Lee's nose and tried to get up. "I want to go drink more and make out on the couch, too."

Lee, bemused and out of his depth, nodded. "Okay." He turned off the water and got towels, wondering when his life had become so weird.

Chapter Seven
Starting Was So Easy

It was well past two in the morning when the party broke up and Tony took Lee back to his rooming house after the initiation. Lee looked around as soon as they stepped out of the door into the driveway, but couldn't see much at all; there was no moon, and the overhang of several trees blocked out most of the surrounding area.

"Do you know where we are?" Tony asked as they pulled out onto the street. The lane itself had been longer than expected, like the house was in the middle of a city block instead of fronting the street. The fences had been high on either side, and overgrown with vines or evergreens.

Lee looked around at the residential neighborhood, at the widely spaced street lamps and the huge homes set far back from the street, surrounded by wide lawns. "Not a clue. Looks like the kind of place that wouldn't want a bunch of college kids hanging around, though."

"That's exactly what I thought, too." Tony seemed pleased with this, as delighted by Lee's reaction as he had seemed at just about every word Lee had spoken all night. He even looked proud when Lee found the hook in the entry with his own name over it, as if finding out where to hang his coat or robe was a big deal. "The street address is hard to find, but once you're walking down the street it'll become obvious where to turn and make your way back to the house."

"It's hidden?" Lee stared at a particularly grand house as they cruised by it, its floodlights showing off Roman columns and what had to be a two story conservatory on the side. "God."

"Some of these places, huh?" Tony nodded as they came to an intersection and paused at the stop sign. "The house isn't hidden, really—it's the guest house for one of these places. Come by tomorrow in the daylight, you'll see."

Lee nodded, but had no intention of running over to check the place out the very next day. There was being pleased to be a part of something and then there was being an over-eager dork.

"There's an unwritten rule," Tony said as the car rolled forward again, "that no one but the new guys go to the house for the week after initiation. So you have time to explore and wander around and figure out where things are before you walk into a room full of people you don't really know."

That brought out a half smile, and Lee nodded again. "Okay. Cool."

Tony drove a much more direct route than he had when bringing Lee there, and the lack of blindfold on the return journey was a help, too, of course, for Lee to pinpoint the location of the house. He turned at the next corner and Lee suddenly knew where they were.

"Dude. We're only about four blocks from campus!" He turned his head and pointed in the opposite direction. "My advisor lives over there a ways. I had to drop off a form there last September and got lost on the way. That means..." Frowning, he looked back toward where the brotherhood had their house. "Wow. We've got some pretty powerful neighbors. Lawyers and politicos and lobbyists and such. Some old money mixed in. How did the brotherhood manage that?"

Tony merely smiled and drove him home.

The first time Lee got a look at the house in daylight was the next morning. He'd been unable to sleep in, despite his late night, and he had to work at three that afternoon. Hopefully it would be his last Sunday shift for a long time; he'd traded with one of his coworkers to work every Tuesday night instead so he could be at the house like Tony had suggested. That Sunday morning, though, he walked through crisp air and nearly deserted streets until he reached the illustrious neighborhood. He saw no one, assumed that nine on a Sunday morning was too early for anyone to be up or they were all off at church, and discovered that Tony was right: he knew where to turn as soon as he saw it, a little ally with tall fences and masses of ivy, leading around the back of yet another mansion.

Then, in the muted yellow light of a January morning, Lee used his house key for the first time.

By the weekend closest to Valentine's Day, a month later, he could find his way there in his sleep, but he was no less awed by it—both its existence and the structure itself. The air was cooler in February, too, but it made the warmth of the huge entry all the more welcoming. Also welcoming was the sight of coats on pegs and shoes piled up along the walls.

It always struck him as a little hobbit-ish, the way they each had a peg and a locker, a space for shoes and bundles. Of course, the fact that they had actual, honest to God, robes added to the illusion. He'd been both dismayed and relieved to find out that they only donned the robes twice a year, though, at initiations and the final meeting of the school year, when the members in their final years at the college would take their leave.

When Tony would leave.

It was February still, he reminded himself as he hung up his coat and shoved his mitts away, and a Saturday night, as well. He couldn't remember the last time he'd had a Saturday night free; probably not since the night of his initiation. Lee slung his backpack over one shoulder and headed into the main part of the house, already smelling coffee and popcorn, hearing a few voices and the click of balls as someone played pool.

"Hey, Lee." Over on one couch Stan and Ken were reading what looked to be the student newspaper, a bowl of popcorn between them. "There's more on the counter, if you want."

"Thanks." Lee put his bag on one of the two library tables they used for studying, eating, planning and everything else. "Maybe in a bit." He didn't want to rush for the food. He didn't want anyone to make note that after a month of coming by the house and soaking up the warmth of both brotherhood and paid utilities, he still had yet to bring much more than a few bags of chips to stock the communal snack cupboards. Instead, he began to pull his books out of his bag. "How come you guys aren't at the dance?" He knew that Stan, at least, had been planning to go to the campus GLBT Valentine's Dance.

"Too early. Jimmy isn't picking me up until nine-thirty." Stan looked at his watch. "Oh, crap!" He jumped up, almost spilling the bowl of popcorn onto the floor. "See you tomorrow."

Laughing, Lee and Ken watched Stan bolt for the door.

"What about you, Lee?" Matt was at the pool table,

taking aim at the eight ball. "Why aren't you getting all pretty for your date? What was his name? Clyde?"

Lee rolled his eyes and crossed to the little kitchenette. "Cyril. How the hell did you know I had a date?"

"I heard you telling Tony last weekend." Matt shrugged and took his shot, which missed. "So why are you here?"

Lee watched him from the counter as he poured the coffee. The house was open concept, with just the one huge room, a galley kitchen and the entry room. The bathrooms—two of them for a house full of college boys—were on the far side, back in the farthest corner. As he poured milk into his coffee and contemplated taking some of the popcorn, Lee said, "The all important Valentine's date got canceled. He said 'sudden family emergency', I say 'better offer'. Whatever. He was pretty, not very bright. I'll do some reading here and kick your ass at pool instead." Truth be told, Cyril was very pretty and very low maintenance, but there hadn't been enough interest on either side for more than the occasional blow job.

Matt grinned at Lee. His curls were peeking out from under his ball cap and he looked both adorable and slightly manic, like the kind of kid who you just knew was going to get you in trouble but you didn't care because it would be just so much fun to get there with him. "You know, most people would be insulted to be your second choice."

Lee winked at him. "But not you."

"Nah. Not me. That's because I know you're full of shit. I'll totally kick your ass and you know it."

"Not until after I get through a chapter." Lee took his mug and went to the table, glancing up and nodding as the outside door opened and closed again. "Hey, Echo."

"Hi. God, it's cold out there." Echo came in, shivering,

and made his way directly to the coffee pot. "What's up?"

Lee held up his notebook. "Paper for Poli-Sci 124b. And then kicking Matt's ass at pool."

Matt nodded and finally sank the eight ball. "C'mon, Echo. You can warm up over here and show him how to play."

Echo snorted. "Right. I've seen you play, Mr. Lewis. I'm not getting into that. Tip for you—don't try to hustle a hustler. Keith, Dale, and Leon all told me about you the week after you came to us. You might have wanted to be a little less obvious."

Matt merely laughed and shook his head. "We're brothers now, man. I figured y'all would want to know where you stood right off the bat."

Snorting, trying not to smile, Lee sat down and rummaged in his bag for a pen. Matt had a point, really, and had been an open book since the moment they'd met. A sunny, warm, wide open and scarily honest book. Lee wasn't sure if it was endearing or terrifying.

Echo seemed to have already decided in Matt's favor and was looking at Matt fondly. "Let me warm up my fingers and steal a few minutes on the couch with Ken. Rack 'em up, though."

Matt racked, Echo took his coffee to the couch, and Ken, who had been mostly silent since Lee's arrival, put down the paper and made room before the two of them started talking in low tones.

Lee read and made notes, smiling to himself. If he noticed anything at all, it was that he found it surprisingly easy to study there, with other people around. His own room in the rooming house was certainly never as conducive to thought and concentration.

Others came and went over the course of the evening, and Lee made it through two chapters between rounds of pool with Matt and whoever wanted a turn. He ate a little, got into a long discussion with Keith, who was the sophomore ahead of Lee in their little segment of TCF, about the record book and what was expected of them in their junior year at college. It was comforting to know that Keith was as awed by the whole concept of being in charge of the records as Lee was.

Lee was packing up his books and waiting for his next turn at the pool table when Ken approached him, extending a can of soda like a gift. "Here, you look like you earned it. What were you working on?"

Lee took the can gratefully and smiled at Ken. "History, but it was all a ruse. That was the easy homework; I have stats to do tomorrow and I think it might break me."

"Yeah?" Ken shrugged one shoulder. "I can give you a hand, if you want. I'm good with stats, got great grades when I took it."

"Really?" Lee beamed at him. "That would be awesome. Even if you can give me fifteen minutes, that would be a help. I think I'm missing a basic concept somewhere, and I really, really need to get a grip on this or my career is done and over before I'm nineteen years old. That would be a tragedy."

Ken snorted. "It would, yes. I'll see what I can do." He nodded and then inclined his head toward the pool table. "I'll be here tomorrow afternoon. But for now... want to know what brothers really do?"

Lee's eyebrows shot up to his hairline.

"We act like siblings in all senses. Let's go and kick Matt's ass."

Laughing, Lee followed Ken to the pool table for a little two on one. He thought maybe having brothers was going to work out just fine for him.

By one in the morning most everyone had gone again, saying they'd be back for the usual Sunday afternoon gathering, and it was just Matt and Lee, cleaning up the kitchen and putting dishes away.

"Want a lift home?" Matt offered, drying the last glass. "I've got my Jeep, but I'll warn you—the heater's busted. I'll get it fixed in a day or so, if I can get to my buddy's garage when his dad's around to let me use his tools. For tonight, though, it's a chilly ride."

"Better than no ride and a long walk home." Lee drained the sink and nodded. "Thanks, I appreciate the offer."

They made sure the lights were all off and left, locking the door behind them. The ride home was, as promised, not warm, but at least it was faster than walking, and Matt knew the town well enough that Lee only had to tell him what street and block to go to.

"This is pretty close to school. Sweet."

"It's not bad." Lee pointed out the house, sighing when he saw all the lights still on and people out on the porch smoking cigarettes. "Looks like a party. Again."

"Dude." Matt pulled up to the curb. "At least in the dorms there's quiet hours. Are you going to be able to sleep with all this going on?"

Lee watched two of his housemates wrestle each other to the ground next to a frozen puddle. "Yeah. I've got ear plugs and my door locks."

Matt shook his head and looked vaguely amused. "Okay, then. Hey, want me to pick you up tomorrow? I figure with a full house gathering and all it might be a good idea to get there around lunch time or so, stake out the table for homework."

"You mean the pool table."

"No, man." Matt laughed. "I do have homework, and Tony said he'd help me with my English composition paper."

"He's good that way." Lee smiled and opened the car

door. "That'd be cool, thanks. My room's on the second floor, top of the stairs. Has a four painted on it. Just knock when you get here."

"You got it. Have a good night."

Lee waved and headed inside, stepping over a leg and ignoring invites from the partiers to join in. He had to be careful not to accidentally clock anyone on the head with his backpack as he went up the stairs; the party seemed to be spilling out all over the house.

His room, though, was blessedly free of people and noise, thanks to a strong lock and the earplugs he'd purchased during his first seventy-two hours as a resident in a rooming house. He knew it wasn't ideal, but it was cheap and it gave him a certain amount of freedom. He could put up with too many people in one place, and too much noise. He thought maybe he could put up with anything for a pre-determined length of time. Four years in this case, and only three and a half left to go.

That three and a half years was looking to be a lot warmer than the first half of his freshman year had been, too. He had a place to escape to.

He had people who not only wanted him, but who had sought him out.

With that thought on his mind, Lee settled onto his mattress on the floor and went to sleep, the world muffled from touching him until he chose to let it in.

The room was considerably brighter when he woke up, but he lay on top of the blankets for a few moments, trying to get his bearings. The sun was up, for some reason he hadn't bothered to undress and was tangled in his T-shirt and the long shirt he'd worn over it, and his jeans felt like they'd tried to give him a wedgie all on their own. His ears were sore, and he couldn't hear very well. The floor was vibrating.

If that party was still going on, Lee was going to

complain to the landlord. That was just too ridiculous to be possible. It wasn't until he was sitting up, tugging at his shirt in frustration, that he realized everything was muted due to his earplugs and that the vibration was from someone banging on his door.

"Hang on," Lee called, stumbling to his feet and almost tripping on his backpack. "God, I'm coming." He ripped the earplugs out and started flipping the locks on his door. The deadbolt first, the padlock on the inside hasp, and then the puny little door handle lock.

"Good morning, Scout." Matt grinned at him and thrust a huge cup of takeout coffee into his hand. "I was going to make a joke about you coming, but now I've moved onto you being so paranoid you barricade yourself in."

"Scout. That's funny. Really. Never heard it before in my whole life." Lee realized he only had one eye open and rubbed the other one with the heel of his free hand. "What the hell are you doing here so early? I thought you said lunch time."

Matt's grin grew even wider. "It's ten to, bud. Sorry."

Lee checked the digital clock on his dresser and groaned. "Christ. The whole morning." With a sigh he backed up and let Matt in the room. "God, sorry. And thanks for the coffee."

"Clearly, you need it." Matt came in and closed the door behind him. "Take your time, drink up. You must have been wiped out last night—or did the party keep you up?"

"Nah, I crashed." Lee pointed to the one chair and went to look out the window, pulling back the curtain a little to see bright sunshine and wintery looking air, stained a weak yellow from the sun and dirty window panes. "Earplugs are a gift from God."

"Or American ingenuity."

"Or that." Lee drank his coffee and watched Matt look curiously around his room. This was usually the worst part, the first time someone new saw where he lived and assessed his situation. Sometimes people asked questions, sometimes they were polite but uncomfortable, and sometimes they were carelessly indifferent. Lee had learned a lot about teenagers and young adults by the way they reacted to his obvious lack of material possessions.

Matt fell into the group who seemed not to care either way, his attention almost immediately caught by the textbooks stacked nearest to him. "How come you picked political science?" he asked, reaching for the top one. "It sounds deadly dull to me."

Lee smiled. "Politics is never, ever dull. Power plays, games, wars: it's like history, only we can change it." It was, of course, a lot more than that, but as a conversational quick reply the phrase had become Lee's standard. He drank more coffee, glad it wasn't so hot that it would burn his tongue. Matt must have picked it up on campus, since it had had time to cool. "What's your major, then?"

"Engineering." Matt made a face. "On paper, anyway. We'll see at the end of this semester. I've got to line up my scholarship applications next month and see how my midterm grades are."

Lee nodded. "Mine's a good one, but I have to keep my grades way up there. For sure." Coffee finished, he tossed the cup in his trash and picked out a set of clean clothes and grabbed his toiletry bag. "I'll be back in five minutes, just need to wash up. Make yourself at home, okay?"

"Sure thing." Matt saluted him with his coffee cup and put the text back. When Lee left the room, Matt was checking out the small selection of novels, most of which had been bought second hand and were on the reading list for his required English class. Matt probably had the same ones in his dorm room.

True to his word, Lee was changed, shaved and brushed in a few minutes. When he got back to his room, face a little tender from not enough hot water, he found Matt not looking at a novel but instead sitting with Lee's copy of The Chosen Family's little book.

Matt smiled at him, his face somehow softer than when he was grinning. "Does it ever hit you how amazing this whole thing is? How utterly weird and wonderful it is to be a part of something like this?"

Lee nodded, unable to help smiling back. "I know. I spent the first week waiting for someone to tell me it was all a joke, but the more I saw the more I knew it couldn't be. The enormity of it all, the details—there's history you can just feel. Like, the house. There's no way someone could've set up all that for a joke. So... it's real. And if we accept the very existence of TCF, we accept what it is, all of it. Including the amazing fact that we're a part of it."

Matt was wiggling, nodding at him. "Uh-huh. That." He held up the book. "And this. Mine has notes on one of the pages, in pencil. One of the people in my line left notes to himself about how to do things. He was a part of this God knows how long ago, and he was as nervous as me. Neat."

Lee tossed his dirty clothes into the laundry bag and started packing his books for the day. "It's cool. History and an actual secret society. You know what? I heard rumors that Carrigan Chantz was a member."

"No shit." Matt blinked at him, twice. "Who says he was a brother?"

"Uh, tall guy, a sophomore. Michael. So I looked in the record book, and there he is. You can see for yourself. He was taking psychology." The record book was kept up by the members in charge of Records, which happened to be Lee's line, but anyone at all could read it and look things up. It was locked in a drawer in the house, but the key was in the lock.

"I love his music," Matt said, grinning. "He's from my area, you know. Well, my extended family. North Carolina, man. God's country, unless you're talking to a Texan. But Texas doesn't have keyboard players who can play like that with only nine fingers."

Lee cocked an eyebrow. "You're very random, you know that?"

"I've been told. Man, I need to read that book. That's so cool."

Lee laughed and grabbed the last of his stuff. The record book had been the first thing he'd headed to, after the first rush of being initiated had settled a bit. He glanced at Matt, his head tilted to the side. "What line are you, again?"

"Keys." Matt laughed and then intoned, "Welcoming Brothers and Defending the Door."

"Heh. Cool. Do you know how to do it yet?" The actual responsibility of their lines and positions wouldn't fall to them until their junior year at college. Freshman year was for selection and initiation, senior year they would devote to finding a new freshman to bring to the family. Sophomore year, as far as Lee could tell, was for hanging out and being a brother, and when they were juniors they would do their work, representing their 'bloodlines' in TCF.

"Keys isn't hard," Matt said, flipping through the rule book. "When the seniors leave the year before, they make copies of their house keys and turn them in to me. Then I pass them out at the initiations in January. Pretty simple. Same as for Pins, I guess."

Lee shook his head and tugged at the zippers on his bag. "Nope, Pins is different. Well, the handing them out is the same, but the pins themselves just... appear. In the house, at some point over the winter break. One morning they're just there, four of them on the table."

Matt stared at him. "Really? Says who?"

"Well, Tony. But Ken was right there, and he's the one who handed them out to us this year. He said they were there on December twenty-eighth, when he got back from break early."

Matt was frowning. "That means that either there's another secret we'll learn later, or someone not currently a member of the brotherhood comes in."

"We'll find out someday, I'm sure." Lee picked up his bag. "I'm ready. Sorry I made you wait."

"No problem, really." Matt got up and followed him to the door, then paused. "You know, I didn't even know I was missing anything until I was given this. And only a month later, I'd be a mess if it was taken away from me."

"Yeah." Lee had his keys in his hand, but he stopped to look at Matt, knowing exactly what he meant. "It's pretty big stuff. I mean, it's all a bit of a joke, poking fun at so many things and maybe The Chosen Family isn't even necessary, in this day of GLBT groups for support. But this feels different."

"Tighter." Matt nodded. "There's passwords and over the top cliché stuff, but that's what makes it so fun, you know? And under the fun there's truth. A secret society set up to protect us from what Alexander the Freaking Great was." He snorted and rolled his eyes. "Good enough for one of the greatest warriors in history, but in the twentieth century we had to use his name as a code. They were really very smart."

"I confess that I'm still a little surprised that they came up with such a mishmash of legend and story to be the theme of our society."

"Theme?"

Lee shrugged. "For lack of a better word."

Matt shrugged, too. "Alexander and Heaphesteon were gay, or at the very least bonded to each other in a very profound way and generally assumed to have been lovers. Achilles and Patroclese were as well, and Alexander the Great admired them so much he modeled a lot of his life on theirs. I can see why the two stories were blended for use as a sign and counter sign."

"I'm not sure how historically accurate that is," Lee said dryly. "The effect of mixing up parts of one with parts of the other makes the whole thing rather confusing, I think."

"No one would guess what they were talking about when they were planning, you have to give them that much. They didn't have the privacy we did and had to plan out in the open. We have the house, after all. That came later."

"Did it?" Lee blinked. "When? Who said?" That was the kind of information Lee couldn't get enough of. The history all laid out there was great, but he wanted all kinds of knowledge, if he could get it.

Matt frowned as he thought. "Okay, so, it says in our handbooks that The Society was formed in 1955, and the house became ours to use in 1967. It's still not owned by us, but there's no reason to think that we'll lose it. As long as the brothers keep treating the building and the owner with respect, I'm sure it'll be there for the Family. I guess."

"Who owns it?" Lee leaned forward, pretty sure that if anyone knew Tony would have already told him.

Matt shrugged "If you want a theory, I suspect it belongs to one of the founders."

"That would be clever, like Tony said." Lee winked at him and opened the door, pushing away the mystery. "They set up a way to pass on something really important,

Matt, and maybe taking care of the house is a part of that. They gave us a platform of respect—for each other and for ourselves. We need to live up to it."

"I can do that." Matt followed him out of his room and watched while Lee closed and locked the door. "Mostly by kicking your ass at pool and giving you a ride now and then."

"I'll take it."

"I know you will. Come on, I want to find out if we have any other famous dudes in our family."

Chris Owen

Chapter Eight
R-E-S-P-E-C-T

When Lee woke up, he was sure he was going to die. He had no idea how he could possibly have caught the flu, but clearly he had. His head was pounding, his stomach was a mess, and something might have died in his mouth. Rolling over seemed like a very, very bad idea, so he lay limply where he was, hoping that death would take him almost immediately and he could end his suffering.

Then the memories started coming to him, one after another like a sick and sadistic marching band, complete with drum major. The drinking. The laughing. The eating. The sex, the shower, the more drinking, the coffee and cold water and even the swimming. The sun had been coming up when they'd done that, and he honestly wasn't sure if they'd been naked or not.

Lee groaned and made himself sit up. He had to get up if he was going to make it to the bathroom and the shower. "Oh, God." He whispered it, but an answering curse from the other side of the bed sealed his intention to get up. He couldn't stay in bed with Joey, not when he was still half-drunk and all the way messed up. "Go back

109

to sleep," he mumbled.

Joey made a noise that was either agreement or a death rattle, and Lee dragged himself off to the bathroom.

The flashbacks to sex were a lot stronger in the shower and he wound up leaning on the tiles with his eyes closed, hoping that if he stood there for a while he'd eventually feel human enough to deal with the situation. When the hot water got cool, he turned it off and stayed where he was, drying slowly. His head didn't hurt so much if he stayed still and didn't think too hard.

Eventually, however, he had to get out and find a towel; Joey would need the bathroom, and no one was going to put the coffee on if Lee didn't do it. Also, the pain relievers were in the kitchen—along with all the towels, it turned out. They'd apparently spent some time trying to figure out which towels to take to the pool.

The kitchen was a complete disaster. Clothes, food, bottles, glasses, dishes, and towels were all over the place, and the sink was full of what looked to be tea towels bearing more food and other substances Lee didn't want to think about too hard.

In the middle of the mess were two pairs of soaking wet boxer shorts, so that was one mystery solved.

Deciding that he'd be a good host, Lee first put the coffee on and then found the bottle of pain relievers. He took a couple, drank a lot of water, and then got Joey's ready for him. A big glass of water in hand, he took three pills into the bedroom and set them on the nightstand.

"Hey, you," he said quietly, using one hand to brush hair from Joey's forehead. "Pills and water here. Mouthwash in the bathroom. Coffee is on. Stay here for a while; I used all the hot water so it'll be about twenty minutes before you can shower."

"God, I feel like shit," Joey whispered. He managed to get one eye open, though, and then he attempted a grin that failed about half-way into formation. "You're naked. If I wasn't dying I'd be thrilled."

"The towels were in the kitchen," Lee told him. He would have rolled his eyes, but that would have hurt. "You take these, okay? Rest up a little more and then shower. You'll feel better."

"Are you still going to be naked when I do all that?" Joey's eye had closed again and he was still whispering.

"Probably not."

"Are you going to be naked again in the near future?"

Lee sighed. "We'll talk. When we don't have to whisper."

"Boo." Joey rolled over and groaned. "Gimme an hour. Stay naked. I like it."

Lee laughed softly and walked around the bed to his dresser and found a pair of track pants to pull on. "Meet you in the kitchen. I'll try to find your clothes."

Joey's reply was another mumble, but Lee hadn't expected much more than that. He went back to the kitchen, checked to make sure the coffee was brewing, wished it would brew faster, and set to work.

The towels all went into the laundry, save one that was still folded. That one he put in the bathroom for Joey, hoping it had missed all of the carnage they'd wrought. The clothes were sorted into piles of "belongs to Joey" and "disgusting", the latter being put with the towels. The tea towels in the sink joined the laundry, and then the food was thrown out.

He only had to stop for more water once, and to sit down to hold his head twice. Lee was pretty pleased, all in all; he'd expected to be sick and seemed to have avoided that entirely.

When he heard movement from the bedroom he got up from the table again and took Joey's clothes down the hall. "I'm not sure if you actually want to wear them," he said with a tight grin that he hoped didn't look too much like a grimace, "but here they are."

Joey took the stack, gave Lee a kiss on the cheek and headed into the bathroom without a word.

Lee admired his butt until the bathroom door closed, then went back to scrape plates and gather all the dishes for washing. While Joey showered Lee checked all the bottles, put the empties in the recycling and found the caps for the spirits that were still left. They'd really had a lot to drink, it seemed. Far, far too much.

When the water stopped running in the bathroom, Lee filled the sink and started washing dishes, starting with the mugs. The coffee was ready and they'd need it, as soon as they could get it.

"I think I might live." Joey's voice was rough, but he was speaking at a normal volume as he came into the kitchen wearing only his jeans. "Coffee?" He draped his shirt over the back of a chair.

"Right there. Mugs are clean." Actually, most of the dishes were clean; they'd used a lot of paper towels, but hadn't bothered with many plates. "There's filtered water in the fridge, too."

"Thanks." Joey came up behind Lee and rested his hands on Lee's hips. Pushing close, knee to shoulder, Lee could feel the warmth of the shower still radiating from Joey's bare torso. "I would have helped clean up." Joey pressed a kiss to Lee's shoulder blade.

"I know. But you were busy dying." Lee rinsed the last glass and put it in the sink, but didn't move away from Joey's body.

"Yeah, that." Joey kissed him again. "I. Um, I have a few gaps in my memory," he murmured. "Swimming?"

"Happened. Not naked. I'm pretty sure we didn't yell for Stephanie, either."

A laugh burbled out of Joey's chest. "Oh, man. Now I remember that. Talking about it. That was right before...?"

"That happened, too." Lee was pretty sure Joey knew that. "And then you blew me in the shower."

"Did I earn points for not drowning myself?"

It was Lee's turn to laugh. "Yeah. You earned points just fine. And as far as I can tell, that was all the sex there was—one of us passed out in the bed before the next round, as far as I can remember." Maybe. There was a hazy memory about making out in the pool.

"Probably for the best. We wouldn't have been with it enough to clean up, if we'd managed to get off." Joey kissed him once more and moved away to get coffee. "How do you feel?"

"Incredibly hung over. But I'll live." Lee got the milk from the fridge and then wiped down the counters and table while Joey got the coffee ready. "You?"

"I've been worse, I'm sure, but it's been years." Joey put a coffee cup in front of Lee and sipped from his own. "I asked you out last night, right? I meant to."

Lee paused with his coffee halfway to his mouth and frowned. "Yes, I think so. Something about dinner tonight."

"Right." Joey nodded, and it didn't seem to bother his head. At least, he wasn't wincing. "And you made us both promise not to freak out this morning. Are you freaking out?"

"Nope." Lee wasn't, not really. He knew what he had to do. "And I'll go out for dinner, as long as I don't have to drink. But we need to talk about something." He made himself look at Joey instead of studying his coffee cup. "Damn, this would be a lot easier if you were wearing more clothes."

"Says the man dressed only in a pair of track pants."

Joey walked to him and put his coffee mug on the table. "You'll come to dinner?"

"Yes." Lee, sitting with his legs out in front of him and crossed at the ankle, didn't move. "But not so much as a glass of wine."

"That's fine." Joey took Lee's mug out of his hand and put it on the table as well. "We don't need to drink."

"We're all grown up and everything." Lee didn't take his gaze off Joey, though he did let it drift from Joey's face down over his pecs and abs.

"We are," Joey agreed. His voice had dropped a bit lower, and was still gravel-rough from drinking. He straddled Lee's thighs and settled down to sit on Lee's lap. "What did you want to discuss?"

"So not fair." Lee had hoped that being hung over would give him some immunity from Joey's good looks, but being that close to him was no match for a headache.

Joey grinned and kissed him, his mouth tasting of coffee and mouthwash, far better than beer and pizza. Lee let him in, having no intention of turning down kisses, anyway. Kissing was a good thing, and kissing Joey was an amazing thing.

When Joey moved closer about an inch, though, one hand dropping to Lee's lap, Lee shook his head. "Wait." He kissed Joey once more to prevent hurt feelings and lifted Joey's hand. "I need to tell you a story." He kissed Joey's palm and looked up at his face. "Okay?"

Looking thoughtful and a little surprised, Joey nodded. "Okay," he said slowly. "A story. No making out?"

Lee smiled. "There's no rush, is there?"

"Well, no." Joey smiled suddenly. "No rush. Just want. You're lovely and sexy and I wanted to try it out sober."

"I can understand that." Lee nodded and glanced down. "I really can." He didn't exactly have a rock hard erection, but there was interest, shown off by the track pants. "But no rush. So listen to my story, and we'll see where we are."

"Sure." Joey moved to get up, but Lee kept him in place with a tighter hand on Joey's wrist. "Okay, staying," Joey said with a laugh.

"It's not a long story." Lee smiled and kissed Joey's mouth again. "Remember last night when we were talking and you said that Tony was always feeding people?"

"Sure."

"And I said that I was hungry and that was part of why Tony picked me, I thought? I was kidding, of course, but the truth is that I was hungry, sometimes. Very." He shrugged one shoulder. "My parents died when I was twelve and I went to live with my grandmother. I loved her like mad and she took great care of me, but money was really, really tight my whole life. I got to college on scholarships and bursaries, and worked all the time. Gram was on a fixed income and it was really small. She could keep herself, and I could keep myself, but there wasn't any wiggle room, you know?"

Joey nodded, his eyes thoughtful and sympathetic, but Lee knew the look exactly. Joey thought he knew, and the numbers probably made sense to him, but he didn't really know. In an academic and removed way, Joey got it. He was genuinely sympathetic. But he hadn't ever lived with it, with the lack of food and the utter lack of new clothes for ten years, everything worn bought at thrift stores, other than underwear and sneakers. Lee had been adamant about things like brand new underwear and new shoes, but everything else was fair game. Joey's heart was in the right place, however, and that was all that mattered to the story.

"Tony bought me breakfast every few weeks. He said he was going to take advantage and spend time with me while he could, since he was graduating, see? We hung out at the house, of course, but whenever he could, he'd take me out for a muffin and eggs. He'd make sure, at the house, that he'd made just a little too much of the pasta and he'd send it home with me. That kind of thing. I was his feedee that year. Which was great, don't get me wrong. He never, ever made me feel like he pitied me or that I was a project. I don't think anyone else other than Matt knew I really didn't have enough food, ever."

"He's a good guy," Joey said with a slight nod. "One of the best of us."

"He really is. But more than the occasional meal, which I appreciated—ramen gets dull, man—he did other things for me. He'd find clothes, like if his roommate was throwing stuff out, almost brand new, and he'd give them to me. He was always turning up with something in hand that he'd come across and it was always something I needed." For a while Lee had thought Tony had been taking inventory of Lee's possessions, but Tony just seemed to have a gift for being in the right place at the right time to get things for Lee.

Lee went on. "He taught me a lot in a few short months. He taught me to pay attention to my brothers, and to be open to accepting from them. To listen to advice, to offer it, to let them help me when I needed it, and to respect them enough to pay it forward when I could. Tony really started me on the path of being a good brother; I mean, I was there for four years and he only had me with him for a few months. But he formed the kind of brother I was going to be, if that makes sense. He made me want to be as good as that for René, my Junior."

"Sure." Joey shifted a little, settling a little more securely on Lee's lap. "I learned from Ira the same way, and tried to do that for Echo."

Lee smiled. "Echo was a fantastic brother to me.

Thank you."

That got him a kiss and then another, but Joey didn't try to take them past that. He seemed to know that Lee wasn't done. "So, Tony graduated and you... what?"

"I got a legacy. Or became one." Lee lifted his gaze to the ceiling. "The last meeting of the year, we did our farewell ceremony and sent the seniors out into the world, just like every year. And just like every year, they did their walk around the neighborhood and came back to party down one last time. And around midnight I went looking for Tony, since I wanted to thank him and have a couple of minutes with him to myself."

"Sure." Joey had to know that the last party of the year was a mixed bag of emotions, especially for the Juniors of leaving Seniors.

"I saw him playing pool and headed over, but got waylaid—by Echo, now that I think of it." He laughed and Joey rolled his eyes. "Anyway, I lost Tony and had to hunt for him. I went out to the foyer, and he was there, just around the corner. He didn't see me—I don't think anyone did—but I heard my name and paused. He was issuing instructions to Ken, Matt, and Dale. About me. He told them to keep it up—to make sure I had what I needed. He didn't make me into a charity case, he made it all about respect. He said, 'he's your brother and he's got one need. Some of us need support with grades, some with coming out, some with our love lives and some with just hanging on. But Lee needs clothes and a few things that aren't about to fall apart. That's all. Just keep an eye out, take care of him and you respect him and you don't ever make him ask you for it. And when he says thank you, you say you're welcome. If he tries to pay you back, you let him. If he can help you, ever, you let him. He respects you, you respect him, and you can all help each other. Family takes care of family and we don't play games.' Just like that. All in a rush, like he was worried they'd say no, or tell him to mind his own business."

"What did they say?" Joey asked, voice soft.

Lee chuckled. "Matt said 'Duh,' like Tony was dumb and then kissed him. Dale took it very seriously and asked him what my sizes were. And Ken... Ken was a special case, really. He said I'd be okay and that respect was never an issue where family came into play."

Joey smiled faintly. "I suspect you're trying to tell me something."

Lee nodded. "I like you. A lot. And you're hot and I want to spend time with you."

"I'm hearing a 'but' in there."

"But I think that it wouldn't be very respectful of us to jump into bed again, yet. I had a great time last night. I want to do it again, minus the drinking. But I want to know you better, first."

Joey blinked at him and started to laugh. "Mr. Sutton. Are you saying you want to date for a while before fucking my brains out on the kitchen floor again?"

Lee blushed, but held his ground. "That's exactly what I'm saying."

"That's incredibly flattering." Joey kissed him, almost chastely. "I don't think I've been turned down in such a nice way before. You're going to have to tell me what's okay, though, since I don't think it's very easy to put things back in the box once they've been spilled out. And I spilled a lot last night."

Still blushing, Lee nodded. "I'm hoping that staying sober will help with that. Kissing is okay, of course. Making out on the couch should be a lot of fun, too. But I'm asking that we stay mostly clothed and that if things get carried away we stop before control is completely lost. I want to... to talk and watch movies and hang out and get to know you. I know the important things—you're part of TCF, so I know vital things about your personality and ethics—but I want to know you."

Joey smiled at him, his eyes bright. "Dating. That's fantastic. Okay." He nodded. "Let's do that. You do realize I have to run home and make some phone calls, right?"

"Sure." Lee had to call some people, himself. Like Matt. "Now?"

Joey winked and wiggled, pressing close. "Uh-huh. You do things to me. You tempt me. And after that lovely story about respect, I'd better go before I feed you."

Lee blushed again, his whole body getting warm. "Yeah, you'd better go. Or at least get off of me. Which isn't the same as getting me off."

"I can wait. I think." Joey grinned and kissed him once more before climbing off Lee's lap. "Dinner tonight. I'll pick you up around seven, okay?"

Lee raised an eyebrow at him and asked, "How, exactly, are you going to pick me up? Walk across the yard and lead me back up by the hand?"

"Well, yes." Joey beamed at him. "Too much, do you think?"

Lee rolled his eyes and found it didn't hurt as much as he'd thought it would. The pills and coffee were kicking in. "I'll come up around seven. Where are we going?" He wanted to have some idea of what to wear; he'd have to get the rest of his laundry going almost immediately.

"Do you like Italian?"

"Love it." Italian was safe and comforting and they could talk for a long time over a meal. "Giovanni's?"

"Exactly what I was thinking." Joey drank the rest of his coffee and rinsed out the mug. "I'll see you at seven," he added, pulling on his shirt. "Um. Have you seen my shoes?"

The shoes were found by the door, and several more

moments were spent trading kisses before Joey finally left, taking a lot fewer bottles home with him than he'd arrived with. Lee stood at the kitchen window, watching Joey walk up the yard to the complex, and smiled.

Matt had been right, more or less. Although Matt would probably strongly disapprove of the drunken fumbles and orgasms, he'd be pleased that Lee was doing the right thing in the aftermath. Being honest. Respectful. Giving Joey a chance and being open about where he was coming from. All in all, Lee thought he'd used his best social skills.

Even if his baser urges had been all about getting rid of the hangover, cleaning his house and then spreading Joey out on the bed and finding out if he'd imagined the sound Joey made just before he came.

Lee was still smiling as he finished up in the kitchen and put the dishes away. He really liked that sound of Joey's. He went into his bedroom and made the bed, then went to start the laundry. After that, it was time to get out the books and get some work done.

Except he kept thinking. Remembering. They'd gone swimming, but he only remembered standing in the shallow end, both of them laughing as they tried to hold each other up. Wet skin and loose limbed gracelessness that came from drink, and then there had been the long, slow drag of his erection along Joey's hips.

Oh, yes. There had definitely been messing around in the pool. They'd fallen into the pool shortly after that, kissing and groping, and Lee had sat on the steps, his legs spread wide with Joey between them.

"We should have turned out the lights," Lee had whispered, watching while Joey massaged Lee's cock with the palm of his hand. "If anyone looks out they'll see."

Joey had laughed, giggled breathlessly, and pulled at the waistband of Lee's boxers to bare the head of his cock, just under the water. "They're all asleep."

"God, I hope so." Joey's hand on him under the water had been magic. They'd made out and climbed on each other and rubbed and ground into each other until Lee had thought he would explode.

"Have you ever fucked under water?" he'd asked, and Joey had shuddered against him, his hips driving harder. "I bet you'd climb right on me, if we'd been smart enough to bring rubbers."

They hadn't been, though, and in hindsight Lee was glad, but at the time he'd wanted to drive his cock into Joey's ass, had wanted to feel him open, slick and hot, had wanted to rest, balls pressed up against Joey's butt.

He was pretty sure they'd come in the pool, talking about it.

"Oh, fuck." Lee opened his eyes and looked down at himself, his hand jacking hard and fast inside his track pants. He was sitting at the kitchen table, fucking his fist with his books laid out, ignored.

But he could hear it again, the sound Joey made just before he came. "Yes. Yes!" Lee's hand tightened and his balls throbbed as he shot all over his stomach, his cock jerking hard against his palm. He was breathless, panting and wanting more.

Lee really, really hoped he'd be able to stay respectful.

Chapter Nine
In-Laws and Outlaws

Dinner at Giovanni's was wonderful, and Lee didn't even feel overly peculiar as he walked home from Joey's that night. It was late for Lee, close to midnight, but as he'd slept in he was reasonably sure he could work for an hour or so before going to bed if he really tried. Of course, sleeping in because one had spent the night carousing wasn't quite the same thing as sleeping in to rest, and he was convinced he'd have trouble concentrating, anyway.

After dinner they'd gone back to Joey's house, talking animatedly about books that had been made into movies and dissing all the movie versions. There were two notable exceptions: Dangerous Liaisons and The Secret Life of Bees had both been deemed worthy. Joey had been horrified to discover that Lee had never actually seen The Princess Bride, and that particular discussion had taken up about fifteen minutes and only ended when Lee had kissed him to shut him up.

After that, there had been a lot more kissing and a lot less talking.

Concentrating on political theory didn't seem to be

playing a big part in Lee's weekend, and that was causing him some worry. He had more work to do, a draft to finish, and appendices to complete. He couldn't actually afford, academically speaking, to be distracted by a romantic or physical relationship. Both together could be disastrous.

He could almost hear Matt lecturing him about being ridiculous and gloomy and putting the cart before the horse. And he could hear himself pointing out to Matt that the sheer number of orgasms he'd had in slightly over twenty-eight hours had sapped him of mental powers to a frightening degree. After that, the mental argument grew circular.

When Lee walked into his house, he wasn't very surprised to find the message light on his phone flashing at him cheerfully. He'd talked to Matt earlier in the day for half an hour or so and had been convinced to call Tony. Of course, between time zones and the weekend there hadn't been an answer at Tony's number, and Lee hadn't wanted to just hang up. So he'd left a stammering message that was probably bad enough to send Tony into a panic. He'd made sure that both Matt and Tony's numbers were programmed into his cell phone and had done his very best to forget about how dumb he'd sounded on Tony's machine.

Lee pushed the button on his answering machine and listened to three messages in a row of Tony telling him to call anytime he wanted, day or night, that he'd pick up. After that was a detailed list of the things Tony would be doing at home, the implication being both that Lee could call and Tony would for sure be there and not asleep, and that Tony would really appreciate if Lee would just phone and save him from having to actually do all the chores he was listing off. Each message also included a reminder that Tony was a night owl.

"Here we go again." Lee went to the fridge and got himself a bottle of water, pointedly ignoring the one beer they'd managed to overlook in their overindulgence the night before and then called Joey.

"Don't tell me," Joey said by way of greeting. "You suddenly remembered that you intended to stay the night and you're coming back up."

Lee rolled his eyes and shook his head. He was grinning as well, but Joey didn't need to know that. "Right, that. To mock you more about your fascination with a movie about a princess and a pirate and a farm boy."

"Hey, don't knock the classics, man. I'm getting into bed; are you coming back or not?"

"No." Lee laughed that time. "I just wanted to find out if there's anything you want me to pass on to Tony or not. He called three times tonight and I better call him back."

"You're kidding. Three times? Oh, I get it. He's in a panic. You didn't tell him why you were calling and he thinks you're going to starve."

"Probably. Anyway, I'll call him now and soothe his nerves and tell him I met an amazingly evil doctor. Any messages?"

"Sure." Joey sounded like he was grinning, too. "Tell him I hid it in Diego's garden. He'll know. And you can give him my number, if he asks."

Lee smirked. "What did you hide?"

"None of your business, Eromenos. I'll talk to you tomorrow. Unless you want to—"

"I'm not going to spend the night." Lee sighed dramatically. "You just want me for my hands."

"And your mouth and your abs," Joey agreed. "Night."

Lee couldn't smile any bigger. "Night." He hung up and took the phone to his bedroom, scrolling back through the last few calls to find Tony's number and pressing the button to call him. With the phone between his shoulder and ear, he waited for Tony to pick up and started unbuttoning his shirt.

"Hello? Scout?"

"Good God." Lee laughed softly. "Not you, too. Matt was the only one who called me that."

"Matt hadn't even read the book—he heard it from me first. How the hell are you? Tell me you're okay." Tony was laughing, his voice a little too loud and a little too fast.

"I'm okay." Lee nodded and undid the last shirt button. He was still smiling. His face was starting to hurt from smiling. "I really, really am. I knew you'd freak, I'm sorry."

"I'm not freaked." Tony did tone it down a bit, though. "I'm glad you're okay. Why the hell are you calling me? And have you talked to Matt? What's going on? I've been... well, sort of freaked all day. Shut up."

"Poor Peter." Lee sat on the end of his bed. "Tell him I said sorry."

"Lee says sorry. And hello, I guess."

A second voice, distant, yelled, "Hi, Lee! He was pacing!"

Lee winced. "God, I am sorry. You're such a worrier."

"It's my curse," Tony said mildly. "I'll cope. Where are you?"

"Home, I was out for dinner. I would have called earlier—"

"I meant where." Tony laughed at him.

"Oh!" Lee made a face. He disliked misunderstanding simple questions. "I'm doing my PhD at Legacy. I know, I should be done by now, but I'm not."

"Who says you need to be done by a specific time?"

Tony brushed the whole thing aside. "You let me know when they hand over the sheepskin, all right? I'll come by and take you to lunch."

Lee had to smile. "I'd like that. I would."

"Good. And don't make me wait a million years. So. Why did you call?"

Lee's cheeks hurt again as his smile grew into the grin he'd been wearing all day. "Do you remember a guy from college named Joey Reed?"

There was a short pause. "Yeah. Yeah, I do." By the second "yeah" Tony sounded more sure. "Hottie into the hard sciences. Biology? No, chemistry. Smart as hell, always happy. Like a ray of sunshine walking into the house."

Lee giggled. An honest to God, couldn't call it a laugh at all, giggle.

"Oh, man." Tony got it, and Lee could tell the moment it sank in. "You two didn't overlap, did you?"

"Nope!" Lee threw himself back on the bed. "He says hello."

"How did you find him?" Tony demanded. "Hang on, I need to move. Sorry, Pete."

Pete's reply was muffled, but Lee was fairly sure he was merely grumbling in a good natured way. Tony and Pete had been together forever; a little thing like a private conversation about college buddies wasn't going to be an issue. Besides, Pete probably wanted to go to bed.

"You never told Pete about TCF?" Lee asked curiously. They'd talked about it, back when Lee was in his sophomore year and Tony had come back for Homecoming. "Not ever?"

"No. I finally had to tell him something, so I was as honest as I could be. Secret society, I took my word seriously, there could be weird things in the future. But nothing that would ever damage my relationship with him, in any sense. He trusts me."

"Good," Lee said softly. Tony deserved that. Everyone did, he supposed, but Tony had earned it so many times over that Lee would probably damage anyone that stood in the way of Tony's happiness. "You know what? I think I've turned out to be fiercely loyal."

"Of course you have." Again, Tony disarmed him with the simplicity of the statement. He'd done that routinely at school. "It's a good look on you. Tell me how you found Joey. At school?"

"No, actually." Lee filled Tony in on the arrangement of Meadowlark Court and how he'd found Joey's pin. "Then I came home and spent, like, half an hour trying to figure out what to do. I panicked a little."

"What did Matt say?" Tony asked thoughtfully.

Lee snorted. "What makes you think I called Matt?"

"Don't play me, boy." Tony laughed at him. "What did he tell you?"

Lee sighed. They all knew him too well to play games, even if the games were silly and fun. "He said I needed to stop over-thinking everything, and let Joey do what he was going to do. Hang out, talk, get to know him. Basically, don't make assumptions and welcome a new friend into my life."

"Sounds like good advice to me." Lee could almost see Tony nodding in approval. "Were you having insecurity issues again?"

"Again? Still." Lee shrugged. "It's not going to go away, Tony. Everything was formed too early and too deeply for me not to have this... this... thing in me. But I can shove it aside. I did."

"Good for you." Tony's voice had dropped to a soft tone, a little bit too close to sympathy. "So when was this?"

"A week ago. Joey gave me space—turns out he called

his Senior and was told to keep it calm until he got a signal."

"Joey..." Tony sounded thoughtful, then he chuckled. "Joey was a very enthusiastic guy."

"No kidding." Lee turned his head and looked at the pillow Joey had used the night before. Enthusiastic was a good word. "He's got this thing about movies—talked for about an hour tonight."

"Cool." Tony had completely lost the nervous energy he'd had when he answered the phone. "That is so cool, Lee. All of it."

"That's what Matt said." Lee smiled. "It is, really. We've got all this history and we didn't even know it."

"How is he doing? He's a chemist? He's happy?"

"Yeah. He's happy." Lee made himself sit up and then go to turn off the overhead light. "He's working for a big company, has a nice place, friends. He's happy and fun and relentless."

"Pardon?" If it was possible to hear an arched eyebrow, there it was. "Relentless?"

"Um." Lee grinned and got back on the bed, his house dark and cozy.

"Harper Lee. Are you sleeping with a brother?" Tony sounded like he was actively trying to be more shocked than amused.

Lee's eyebrows shot up and he snorted. "Wow. Hi, Dad."

"Oh, stop that. So? Are you?"

"There was a close call and it depends on definitions, I suppose. If I were a president, you'd want to see the dress. He got me smashing drunk, we messed around, and now we're dating. I put up some rules about sex; no naked, no orgasms."

Tony choked. "Are you serious?"

"About which part?" Lee was having a hard time not

losing it completely. He felt positively giddy. "Actually, yes. All of it. We got hammered. Drunker than I've been in years. There was drunken fooling around that was very good, thank you very much, despite the drink. And then, this morning, over coffee, I laid out my rules." He grinned. "There's this thing called respect, see, and a story about milk and a cow."

Tony laughed at him, the choking turning into chuckles. "You like him."

"I do." Lee nodded. "I didn't think I would, not this much." He frowned a little, trying to bring back his first impressions, now buried under the energy of mutual attraction and chemicals being released in his brain. "I thought maybe he'd be hung up on stuff like brands and matching dinette pieces and who painted the art on the walls. A silver spoon baby."

"Lee," Tony said gently. "You're hung up about that stuff."

"Because I don't have it." Lee nodded. "I know. I understand my neurosis, I just can't control it. But so far, Joey doesn't seem to care about that stuff much. We'll see what happens when he figures out I'm not only broke but proud; he's not going to be able to take me expensive places until I can afford to take him to expensive places. Or at least, not often. Which means his lifestyle might get hijacked."

"You really do jump ahead a lot, don't you?" Tony laughed again. "How long have you been dating?"

"About twelve hours now." Lee grinned at his ceiling. "I can tell you this stuff. You and Matt. It's not like I'm going to tell Joey, not this way."

"How are you going to tell him?" Tony asked curiously.

"I'll just make suggestions about things to do and places to go—oh, and there's also the sheer amount of time I need to work, both here for my lodging and on my dissertation. This could all go up in the flames from never seeing each other and not having sex."

"You're a hard man to date," Tony agreed. "Busy and manipulative. Good thing you're also a keeper."

"Aw." Lee smiled to himself. "You say the sweetest things."

"I can't help myself. But if you wait years before calling me again, I'll take it all back. Hey, can I have Joey's number?"

"Depends."

"On what? Do you think I'm going to call him up and ask about his intentions with my Junior?"

"Yes." Lee laughed, nodding. "That's exactly what I think."

"Don't be ridiculous." Tony was laughing again, too. "Joey and I actually had two years together, you'll recall. We were friends long before you got your hands on him. In fact, I have stories I can tell you..."

"Oh, a bribe. Nice. I like it. Got a pen?" Lee waited while Tony got himself a pen and then rattled off Joey's number. "He said I could give it to you, if you asked," he added.

"When should I call?"

"When I'm busy working." Lee shrugged. "Whenever you want, Tony. It's all good. He'd like to catch up." He paused. "Me, too. I've missed you."

"Missed you, too, Scout."

Lee was glad the lights were out; it was easier to be sentimental in the dark. "I'll talk to you soon, okay? And we'll keep that lunch date."

"You know we will. Night, Lee."

"Good night, Tony." Lee hung up and put the phone on his nightstand, then finished undressing. He fell asleep with his face buried in the pillow Joey had used, catching

the fading scent of pool water and takeout Chinese food.
    It made for interesting dreams.

Chapter Ten
Work and Games

It had been a long time since Lee had been in anything remotely like a relationship, and months since he'd even had a date. The last date he'd been on had ended when a third party swept onto the scene and scampered off with the guy Lee had just taken to a movie. Having already realized that a pretty face and some knowledge of world geography wasn't enough to make the guy actually interesting, Lee hadn't been heartbroken.

The result of having his head suddenly turned toward the sunshine, however, was that Lee spent two days with his head in the clouds, halfheartedly trying to bring his focus back to his work. By noon on the first day, he'd realized that if he wasn't going to get actual words down, he'd better do his other job in full. With a pen and a few pieces of blank paper shoved into his back pocket in case he got inspired, he slapped on some sunscreen and went out to tend all the window boxes.

Window boxes. Lawn edging. Pool maintenance. Sweeping the decking. Fixing one doorbell, painting trim on two units, tightening a hand railing and, finally, hosing off the deck furniture around the pool, until it was suppertime on Tuesday and he'd written down exactly three sentences.

Of course, within that same two days he'd also talked to Joey for four hours, finding out all about Joey's sister and her kids and also about Joey's work and what he loved and hated about it. They'd had a protracted discussion about what color the pool water really was, and if it was possible to add too much salt to the salt water filtration.

Halfway through Lee's explanation about how the salt water system really worked to kill bacteria, Joey had pounced him and they'd lost track of the conversation. Again.

For two people who weren't sleeping together, they spent a lot of time kissing and panting dirty talk into each other's ears. Lee kind of liked it, although it did make him doubt how long he'd be making Joey wait. It also occurred to him, later when he was jerking off so he could fall asleep, that he was just as much of a tease as Joey was, and that they were both pushing buttons and putting the brakes on.

It was probably the best foreplay Lee had ever had.

He wound the hose up and went to sweep the puddle of water away, ruefully aware that once again he'd stopped thinking about his dissertation and had gotten himself to a state where he'd have to go inside if he wasn't careful. Setting his mind firmly on something non-Joey related, Lee began to plan his evening. A phone call with Joey, a polite decline of any invitations to hang out, and then five hours of work on his dissertation. He could do that.

"Hey, you. Pool boy. I need servicing."

"Pervert." Lee laughed and looked way up to Joey's balcony. "You're home early today."

"Yeah, a lab finished up and we whipped through the meeting. A couple of people are staying to process data, but I'm done until tomorrow morning. Might be working late on Thursday, though."

Lee nodded and lifted a hand to shade his eyes. "Okay. I'll try to live."

"It'll be hard, I know."

Lee smirked. Joey smirked back. They both knew what they were talking about.

"Want to come in for supper?" Joey asked. He was leaning over the ledge, still in his work clothes. His company didn't go for business casual, and he wore button down shirts and ties under his lab coats. Lee thought it was insanely hot. "I can offer you a lovely taco salad."

Lee smiled and shook his head. "I shouldn't. I'm falling behind and really need to work. I'm sorry."

"Ah, well." Joey sighed and shook his head. "Your loss." He was smiling, though, and the words didn't sting. "Hey, can you come up tomorrow night for a while, though? I've got some people coming around for our monthly night of board games. We don't play all night—everyone leaves around ten. Just a glass of wine, snacks, and family-style fun."

Lee squinted. "Are they family?"

"No, not really. In any sense of the word. Just friends."

"Is Bernie going to be there?"

Joey barked a laugh. "Hell, no. Come on, say yes. I'd like you to meet them. Well, actually, I just want you here 'cause you're hot and I might finally win if you distract them."

"Ah, I see your cunning plan."

"I just told you my cunning plan." Joey grinned. "If I leave you alone for the rest of this evening, will you come? You'll have Thursday to bury yourself, too."

Lee nodded. "Yeah, okay. Could be fun. No funny stuff, though." He waggled a finger at Joey. "I am immune to your powers of seduction."

"Sure you are." Joey stood up. "Stay where you are, I'm coming down."

Lee smirked. "Uh-huh."

"We'll see how immune you are." Joey vanished into his bedroom and Lee very briefly considered dashing to his cottage, since he wasn't immune at all.

Before he could go, however, as if he really would, Joey's kitchen door opened and Joey came out, hands in his trouser pockets, tie still neatly knotted. "Hi, there."

"Hi." Lee leered and gave Joey a long look up and down. "Don't get too close; I've been working outside all day and I'm filthy."

"I like it when you're dirty. Are you hot and sweaty?"

Lee watched Joey walk to him and made himself stand still as Joey got right into Lee's personal space. "Hot and sweaty," Lee confirmed. They were just about the same height, and Lee smiled as Joey's eyes dilated. "And probably a little stinky."

Joey shook his head. "Kiss me. Then I'll go eat taco salad and watch TV and think about you. What are you going to do?"

"Curse your name for distracting me again." Lee grinned at him. "While I jerk off in the shower. Then I'll eat and get to work. What time are you going to go to bed?"

"Before you. Kiss me, damn it. If you take a break before eleven, phone me."

Lee kissed him, leaning forward the two inches necessary to bring their mouths together. He licked at the corner of Joey's mouth and kissed him again, smiling as they both kept their hands to themselves. The only point of contact was their lips, and possibly the soft brush of their groins when Joey swayed forward. "I'll call," Lee said softly, pulling away. "You know I will."

"I know no such thing. I remember losing whole days to my work when I was doing my PhD." Joey reached out, then, one hand on Lee's bicep. "It's okay if you forget. Swear."

"I'll call."

Joey smiled and kissed him again, then turned around to walk back to his door. "Stop watching my ass."

"I'm not watching your ass." Lee grinned and watched Joey's ass.

"Sure, sure. See you tomorrow."

"Bye." Lee waited until Joey had gone inside, then turned around to finish the very last of his clean up.

Across the pool area, another door opened and Stephanie stepped out of the other corner unit. She'd obviously been home from work longer than Joey had, as she'd had time to change into shorts and a T-shirt. Her hair was up in a ponytail and she had a knotted trash bag in one hand. "Hi, Lee," she called, walking to one of the recycling bins. "How are you?"

"Fine, thanks. Nice day."

"It is." She tossed the bag and walked to the edge of the pool, taking off one of her flip-flops to test the water. "Is it safe to swim now?"

"Sure is." Lee held onto his broom and nodded. "I adjusted the chemicals a couple of hours ago, and the skimmer's been cleaned. It should be fine."

"Thank you." She smiled at him and wiped water off her foot, then slipped her shoe back on. "Are you going to take another late night dip?"

Lee stared. "Pardon?"

Her smile grew sly, and she cocked her head at him as she walked back toward her kitchen. "Just asking. No reason. Night swimming is often nice, you know."

"Oh, God."

She was laughing as she went back into her house,

her ponytail mocking him. For a nice married lady, she was potentially evil. Lee stared hard at her door, trying to convince himself that she hadn't meant what she clearly did mean.

"Oh, God!" He put the broom away and fled, determined not to ever think about it again.

The best he could manage, however, was to blush his way through making his supper, horrified that he and Joey had been so dumb as to get off in the pool of all places, and equally as horrified that the memory of it still had the power to get him hard. Apparently an audience wasn't a turn off to him. Not sure what to do with that particular piece of self-discovery, Lee ate his supper and turned his attention to his next chapter.

It took reading back several pages to bring his mind back into gear, but he was grateful to find that a few days off hadn't signaled the end of his academic career. He made a few notes, read a few things over to clarify his position, and got to work. Both computer and pen grew warm as he outlined his argument for the next chapter and made a list of his sources; by the time he realized he was both thirsty and at a good place to take a break, it was nine-thirty.

He called Joey as promised, but even Lee had to admit that after a few quick exchanges of "How are you" and "What are you doing" he was itching to get back to work. Joey just laughed at him, extracted a promise that Lee would try to come for games the next night, and let him go.

Lee wasn't sure if it was actual inspiration that pushed him through the next several hours or fear of wasting more time; he decided not to examine his motives too closely and kept on going until his eyes burned and he became less than sure he was making his points concisely or with any insight.

In the morning he put on a fresh pot of coffee, made sure that all of his phones were within reach in case of an emergency, and went right back to work. It felt good, like he'd gained a new perspective, and at noon he called his advisor to set up an appointment to go over the plans for the last few chapters. There would be revisions and a lot of indexing to do, and he'd have to polish the final draft to within an inch of its life, but if he could keep up his momentum Lee was suddenly sure he'd see the end of the process within the year.

Buoyed by the thought, he had a fast sandwich and kept going. At times he paced the kitchen, a page of notes in his hand as he tried to find words to persuade. At other times he put articles in a row on the kitchen floor, then made his arguments about each one, in order. He hoped he'd never have to explain that method of outline to anyone; it was effective for him, but hardly something he'd be happy telling the world about. Great minds didn't need to lay out visual cues on their kitchen floors.

The phone rang just as he was writing what he hoped was to be the final page of the chapter, so he ignored it. He didn't care if it was his land line, his cell, or the Court's cell; he was working and nearing done. He didn't care if the pool had a tree in it, or if someone's banister had come off the wall. He'd take care of it later.

He typed. He actually typed faster, starting the concluding paragraph, and his phone rang again.

"Go away," he muttered. "Busy." Two more sentences. One. "Done!"

Lee hit the key combination to save the chapter and put his USB drive in the computer to copy the file. And his phone rang again, the landline, he finally noticed. Rolling his eyes, Lee scooped it up and answered. "Hello?"

"Hey, it's me. Everything okay down there?" Joey sounded a little concerned.

"Hey, yeah. Everything is good, I was just finishing the chapter." Lee backed up the file and stood up, his back aching. "Oh, man. That's better. Hi."

"Hi." Joey laughed softly. "You got lost, huh?"

"Yeah, I guess. What time is it?"

"Almost eight. I thought you were standing me up."

"Oh, shit." Lee looked at the clock and winced. "I'm sorry. I got caught up and just—"

"I'm teasing!" Joey interrupted. "Honestly, I am. I shouldn't do that. It's okay. You're done now, though?"

Lee nodded. His kitchen was a total disaster, with notes and articles and books all over the place. "Yeah, I'm done. Let me just.... Well, a shower will take too long and I'm clean. Let me change my clothes and I'll come right up."

"Great." Joey sounded pleased. "See you soon. We won't keep you long, I promise. Just have a glass of wine or something and say hi. You must be exhausted."

"Buzzing, actually. Finishing a chapter is like a high." Now that his back wasn't aching, the idea of going up to see Joey was more and more appealing. He wondered if he could get the other people to leave almost immediately.

"I remember that feeling." Joey paused, perhaps wondering the same thing. "Come up and see me."

"Be right there." Lee hung up and went to find clean clothes. He put on his best jeans, his favorites not because they were new, but because he was fully aware of how they fit, and the first T-shirt he saw. Over that he wore an open, button-up cotton shirt, and hoped that he wouldn't be underdressed. If he was, he told himself, he could take solace in the fact that Joey was going to want to jump him on sight.

On his way up the hill, Lee gave himself what amounted to a pep talk. He reminded himself that the other people who would be there were Joey's friends. He told himself that they weren't going to stay very long. He could also leave at any time, and, more to the point, could come back after they'd left and were therefore out of the way so he could kiss Joey a lot. The main thing, he told himself, was that they weren't existing merely to annoy him, they were humans whom Joey liked.

Joey liked him, too, and it wasn't anyone's fault but Lee's that he'd put rules in place and finished another chapter so unexpectedly. It was, in short, his own damn fault that he'd likely die of blue balls.

"Don't be cranky at the nice people," he murmured to himself as he reached Joey's back door. He knocked once, fairly loudly, and went into the kitchen.

The sound of many voices came from the dining room, and Lee closed the door behind him, hearing Joey excuse himself. It was nice that he came running, Lee thought with a smirk.

"Hey," Joey said happily, coming into the kitchen, the door swinging behind him. "Oh. Hi, there." He'd blinked and then leered. "Finished a chapter. I remember that look."

"Come here." Lee grinned at him and toed off his sneakers. "Just for a minute."

Joey was already moving. "Nice jeans."

"I thought you might like them." Joey was coming right at him, fast enough that Lee unconsciously braced himself to take the impact when Joey pressed into him. "Picked them out special."

Sure enough, Joey pushed up close and then closer until Lee had to take a step back and lean against the door. "You should wear them all the time." Then Joey kissed him, tongue plunging into Lee's mouth.

Lee kissed him back, his hands going to Joey's ass and squeezing. Joey had jeans on, too, and a T-shirt, so Lee'd gotten the dress code right. Lee really didn't care right then, with Joey kissing him, one hand in Lee's hair and the other dangerously close to Lee's rapidly firming erection.

From the dining room a voice called, "Hey, Joey? Can you bring more chips when you come?"

Joey snickered and broke the kiss. "Sure," he called out, then kissed Lee again. He was flatteringly breathless. "Tell me you're not going to run out in an hour."

"If I do, it's 'cause I can't sit still and I'll be back."

Joey groaned and stepped away. "Unfair. I can't bail."

Lee merely grinned and thumped his dick, hard, to get it to go down. "Your guests want chips."

"Yeah, yeah." Joey looked him up and down again and made an approving sound. "Damn. You can just hang out here and look pretty all you want, okay?"

"Let me bring my work and you're on." He grabbed a bag of chips from the selection on the counter and held them up. "Why do you have six different kinds of chips?"

"Five. People have their favorites." Joey shrugged and picked up a different brand. "You can, you know. If you want."

"Can what?" Lee opened the bag and ate a chip.

"Come up here to work. Or read and make notes, whatever. I don't watch a lot of TV, just read, myself. If you want to keep notes spread out instead of packing up all the time, you can take over the guest room."

Lee took another chip and thought about it while he chewed. "You're serious."

"Sure."

"Joey! It's your turn! Stop making out with your mystery man and feed us!"

Lee smirked. "I'd better be the mystery man."

"Nah, I have a collection." Joey leaned forward, kissed

his mouth and then tore open the other bag of chips. "Think about it. Offer stands. Come on." He took Lee's hand and they went into the dining room.

Five heads turned in unison, all of them smiling and all of them looking at Lee with various levels of expectation, curiosity and anticipation. Three men and two women, and at least one of the guys looked vaguely familiar.

"Everyone, this is Lee. Lee, these are my friends. Uh, that's Robert, he works in the lab with me. Felix, also a chemist, different lab. His wife, Grace. Jasmine is my buddy from my last job and I kept her 'cause she's cool. And Dan is on the administration end of things at work, but is nonetheless a cool guy. He's our mole."

Everyone smiled and nodded, and Lee used his assorted tricks to remember their names. He shook hands with both Robert and Felix who were closest and also offered their hands; Dan looked like he would have, but Jasmine was distracting him with her breasts. They were very nice breasts.

"Hi, Lee," Grace said, smiling broadly. "It's great that you found the chips, since plainly Joey needs help with those kinds of things."

Joey rolled his eyes and passed her one of the bags. "Hush, you."

On the table in front of them was a game board that Lee had seen only on commercials. "I don't know this one," he said, pulling up a chair. "Who's winning?"

"The girls." Robert pointed to Dan. "He's distracted. Felix likes it when Grace wins. And Joey's been in a fit of nerves; maybe he'll calm down now."

Joey blushed and sat down. "You can hush, too."

"I think it's sweet." Jasmine reached over and patted Joey's hand. "And I think we're kicking your butt so effectively it won't matter if you suddenly get your groove back."

Lee snickered, his attention split between noticing the way Dan was focused on the breasts now brushing his arm and the way Joey was trying to get everyone to shut up and play the game.

"You knew this was going to happen the first time you asked him to come and meet us," Robert pointed out. "I'm impressed you decided to get it over with so soon. I mean, you weren't like this a week and a half ago when he was here."

Lee looked at him, fast, and then tried to picture him wearing a tux. "Oh, right," he said with a nod. "I thought you looked familiar." He looked at Felix and tilted his head. "And you look familiar, but you weren't here."

"He's got one of those faces," Grace said with a smile. "What do you do, Lee?"

Robert reached for his drink. "He's the handyman."

Lee's eyebrows shot up and he looked at Joey.

"Actually," Joey said smoothly, "Lee's a doctoral candidate in political theory. He's going to control our lives from behind the curtain, so do try not to be insulting, Bobby."

Robert blinked twice. "I wasn't—Oh. I was, wasn't I?"

"Foot in mouth disease," Jasmine said in a stage whisper. "We only let him out to play with adults once in a while. What do you say, Robert?"

Lee wasn't sure if he should be amused or horrified, but Robert looked stricken, and Joey looked more than a little uncomfortable. No one else seemed to have anything to say, so Lee made a conscious choice to assume good intent.

"Actually," he said slowly. "Robert is also correct. While I'm finishing my degree I'm also working my way through to avoid masses of student debt." He shrugged in what he hoped would be a humble, self-deprecating way that looked like he was trying to be humble. "In exchange for my house, I'm the property manager and I do the upkeep around the complex. It's a good deal for me and allows me a lot of time to study and write."

Dan, thankfully, seized on that. "I could have used a deal like that when I was doing my degree," he said with a nod. "Would have saved me about twenty grand, maybe. Per year."

Joey handed Lee a wine glass. "Red or white?"

"Red." The no drinking rule had gone out the window and Lee figured he'd just earned his glass of wine. "Thank you."

Still looking abashed, Robert cleared his throat and picked up the dice. "Sorry I was so... thoughtless," he mumbled. "I didn't mean to sound like I was putting you down."

"It's okay," Lee said, arming himself with wine and a bag of chips. "So. Show me how your game is played. I need to cheer Joey on and see if I can turn the tide. To make up for being late, and all."

Joey beamed. "Another chapter done, though. I'll forgive you for being late if it's getting you closer to your doctorate."

That was met with a round of approval, which Lee politely acknowledged. Then, using the guise of studying the game as an excuse to be quiet, he sat back to let them play.

He wished he had continued to ignore the phone ringing, or that Joey had waited a year or so before wanting him to meet these people.

Chris Owenegment>

Chapter Eleven
It's All in the Timing

True to his word, Joey ushered the last of his friends out the front door before ten p.m. after two hours of dice, laughing and teasing. Lee had done his level best to be a good guest and to charm Joey's friends, but it had been hard to come back from the awkward start.

"That could have been worse," Joey told him. He'd locked the door behind Felix and Grace and was walking back to where Lee still sat at the dining room table, crumpling a napkin in his hand. "Someone could have asked how old you are, or how much money you make a year." He rolled his eyes and offered his hand to Lee. "I'm sorry."

Smiling a little, Lee took his hand and allowed himself to be pulled up. "It's not your fault, is it? There are reasons some people belong in labs, after all. You know. Away from the general public."

Joey laughed and tugged him close. "Are you saying that scientists lack social skills?"

"Well, you don't." Lee slid one arm around Joey's waist and nuzzled at his jaw. "Matt says I have a certain

145

lack in that department, too. I think my shortfall merely failed to match up with his, is all."

"Possibly." Joey nuzzled back, his own hand missing Lee's waist and going right to his ass. "But I haven't noticed your lack of social skills. In fact, your skills all seem exceedingly social to me."

Lee laughed softly and kissed Joey's jaw, just under his ear. "Not everyone gets to see those skills. And you have a particularly smart Senior. That week of space was a very, very good idea."

"You don't seem to need a lot of space right now."

Right then Lee didn't need any space at all. He kissed Joey with an open mouth, pulling him close with the arm he had around Joey's waist. Joey didn't resist, his hands just as eagerly sliding over Lee from ass to shoulder until the two of them began to lose their balance.

"That chapter of yours," Joey asked, his mouth traveling over Lee's neck, one hand in Lee's hair to get the angle just right. "Was it a good one or was it one of the ones you just grit your teeth and power your way through to get it done?"

"It's good." Lee gasped as Joey's teeth dragged over his throat. He could feel Joey's cock through two layers of denim, hard and long. "Came out fast and hard, but it'll hold up to questions. Oh, God. Do that again."

"This?" The teeth scraped.

"No. This." Lee took a shuddering breath and grabbed Joey's hand, then dragged it between their bodies. "Touch me. Please."

Joey moaned and got to work, his fingers fumbling with Lee's button and zipper while Lee got his two cell phones off his belt and out of the way. "I thought we were waiting." Joey said, his hand pushing into Lee's jeans and curling around Lee's cock.

"I can be really stupid." Lee's eyes rolled back in his

head when Joey's palm pushed over the crown of his erection. "Dumb idea, waiting."

"If it makes you feel any better, I'll still respect you in the morning."

"Oh, good." It wasn't the respect that Lee was after, not with Joey's hand sliding up and down his shaft. "Awesome." His legs trembled and he held on tight to Joey so he wouldn't fall over. It was right about then that Lee wondered if maybe there really was a secret handshake Tony hadn't told him about, because Joey was touching him almost exactly the same way Matt had, the one time they'd gotten drunk and wondered what if sex really was better with your best friend. Lee started to laugh, almost hysterically. "Make me stop thinking. Please."

"Come on." Joey let him go, then silenced Lee's whimper with a kiss. "Shh, don't fall apart on me. Just come to bed. We'll do this properly, instead of like we're drunk again. Call it respect."

Lee made himself take a steadying breath. "Sure." He nodded and swallowed, did up his pants at least part way so his dick wasn't hanging out. "You're right." They weren't still in college, after all, and they could show some self-control. Chagrined, Lee realized just how much control he'd lost. "I just—"

"Shh, I said." Joey smiled and kissed him again, his hand looped around Lee's wrist. "Come with me. Stay."

Absurdly, Lee wanted to point out that it was a school night, but he was sure it wouldn't be as funny as he intended, so he kept it back. Instead, he nodded and turned his hand so their palms fit together. "For a while, at least," he said.

"It'll do." Joey smiled at him and they went upstairs, holding hands, just like they were adults who knew exactly what they were getting themselves into.

Lee's erection didn't flag and he certainly didn't hold

back when Joey took him right to the bed and kissed him again, both of them standing next to the wide king-sized surface they were about to rumple. Lee suspected that the mattress was much, much more comfortable than his, but right then all he cared about was the extra space and how much of it they could use up.

"Where were we?" Joey asked, smiling against Lee's mouth.

"You were feeling me up and I was losing my ability to stand." Lee kissed him, both hands on Joey's face. "I suggest we eliminate the possibility of damaging ourselves and just get the undressing part over with."

Joey laughed and started tugging Lee's T-shirt up. "I think we managed to get each other undressed okay the other night."

"Drunk off our asses, so there was no awkwardness at all," Lee agreed. He undid Joey's belt. "It's a good thing neither of us is body shy."

Joey snorted. "Like you'd have anything to be shy about."

Lee rolled his eyes and palmed Joey's cock. "Aw, you're good for my ego." Then he kissed Joey to shut him up, and they fell back onto the bed without getting to the part where they were naked.

Joey moved against him, both pulling him onto the bed and pushing Lee onto his side so they could touch and pet while they kissed, and Lee liked that just fine. Joey tasted good, from his mouth to his neck, and Lee had every intention of tasting more. He wanted to lick at Joey's nipples, and make his way down to Joey's cock for a feast. He would bet a good pizza that he could make Joey beg to be sucked, if he played long enough. Of course, there was every possible danger that Lee would lose his own control and come before Joey did.

A danger that seemed more and more likely as Joey

rolled him again and got on top, grinding down on him.

"I thought we were aiming for naked," Lee said, dismayed at how rough his voice was.

"We are." Joey nodded, but he didn't stop, and his breathing was getting thready. "Oh, man. Right there, yeah?" He moved, his cock a hard ridge next to Lee's. "Yeah. There."

Lee planted his feet on the bed and thrust up. "If you make me walk home in wet jeans—"

"I'll lend you something." Joey's mouth crashed down on Lee's and Lee got his hands on Joey's ass, guiding him to move faster, to push down harder.

At first Lee didn't recognize the loud bang for what it was; it was just another punctuation on what was promising to be a spectacular orgasm. But then it happened again and was followed by both a loud yell and an impressive splash.

"What the fuck?"

"Oh, shit!"

Joey rolled off Lee, cursing a blue streak and they both dashed to the patio doors. So, so close, and Lee wasn't sure but he thought that he might still come, if his clothes rubbed in just the wrong way. He shoved his cock to the side and yanked his zipper up as he followed Joey out.

"What happened?" he asked, joining Joey at the railing of his deck and looking down at the pool. "Oh, man." From a distance he could hear his cell phone ringing, and in the pool was a very large potted tree. "How the hell did they do that?"

"Dunno." Joey looked stunned. His hair was messed up, his pants were undone and he looked like he'd been in mid-fuck. "You'd better..." He waved his hand.

Hoping he didn't look quite so obviously coital, Lee nodded. "Yeah." He leaned over the railing and yelled down to the growing group of tenants, "I'll be right there!

Is everyone okay?"

Stephanie looked up at them from the edge of her patio and nodded. "No one's hurt." She did a double take and covered her mouth, but not before he'd seen her eyes go wide and her sudden grin.

"Dude. Get in your room," Lee hissed at Joey. "Or do up your pants."

Joey fled and Lee rolled his eyes at Stephanie, then went in after him. "I better get down there."

"Yeah." Joey was pacing, running his hand through his hair. He hadn't done his pants back up, though. "I suppose that kind of killed the mood."

Lee snorted and pulled him close for a kiss. "No. But it did end the evening; it's going to take me a while to clean that up, and I'll have to see if there's any damage to the property or the pool. Call me tomorrow?"

"I have to work late," Joey reminded him. "But Friday? We can do something?"

"I'd like that." Lee nodded. "How about a movie? There must be something playing worth seeing, and if not we can rent one." If they were really lucky there wouldn't be a damn thing worth renting, either, and they'd be forced to make out all night.

Joey smiled at him and nodded. "Thanks for coming over to meet my friends."

Lee's phone began to ring again. "I have to go." He kissed Joey again, glanced down to make sure he was all put back together, and rolled his eyes. "I suppose the universe could have been trying to tell us something."

"Sure. Next time we'll ignore it. I was really, really close, man."

Laughing, Lee nodded. "I have to go. Now." He let Joey walk him down stairs and outside, though, grabbing his phones on the way.

The crowd had grown bigger, but oddly enough no

one asked him what he'd been doing at Dr. Reed's at ten-thirty at night. Lee supposed that emergencies happened around the clock, and was just grateful that he wasn't expected to explain anything to anybody. "So," he said, standing on the deck with his hands on his hips, looking down at the slowly sinking tree. "Whose tree?"

"I'm horrified to admit it, but it's mine." Mrs. Clark, a very nice lady of about seventy said with a sigh. "I told them there was no way they were going to get it up onto the deck. Not that way." Her son and grandson looked utterly mortified. Her son still had the rope they'd clearly been using to pull it up with in his hand.

Lee nodded and tried not to laugh. It wasn't going to be easy lifting the damn thing out of the pool, especially as the soil got soaked. "Okay," he said, taking off his shirts and tossing them on one of the chairs. "I'll get in there and lift, you use the rope, and we'll get it on the pool deck for now. Then we'll see about the rest."

Assorted people nodded and called out advice, and Lee did his best not to look over at Joey's deck as he took off everything but his jeans and waded into the pool.

"You know," Stephanie said, grinning at him and looking particularly thoughtful. "Jeans get really heavy when they're wet. You could drown."

Lee rolled his eyes. "Nice try. Where's your husband? He's big and strong and could probably lift this thing out with one hand."

"Working," she said sweetly. "You'll do fine."

Deciding to ignore her or risk embarrassing himself, Lee managed to get the tree to the side of the pool where a cluster of people grabbed hold. Mrs. Clark's grandson hopped into the pool with him, and within a few minutes the tree was back on damp land. It was awkward and moderately horrible, since the clay pot had saturated fairly quickly and weighed about nine million pounds, but they'd done it.

Lee got out of the pool and listened to a round of explanations and the story that surrounded what had happened, tuning most of it out. There were too many people trying to tell him, so he used the part of his brain that had attended countless lectures to filter out all but the pertinent facts. When he had a clear picture of what had happened, he examined Mrs. Clark's deck to make sure it wasn't damaged, told her he'd have someone come to double check the stability of the supports, and then sent everyone back to their homes. It was late and getting later; they really didn't need to stand around to watch him skim the pool, treat the water, and go all around the edge to check for broken tiles.

It was well after midnight by the time he was done, though he'd had an audience for most of it. He knew that Joey had watched for a while, because Lee had looked, and Mrs. Clark's family stayed to the bitter end, though she herself had gone to bed. Still, it was almost interesting work, and certainly more exciting than trimming the lawn.

He could have lived without the paperwork he'd have to do and the lack of sex, however. He had dreams about water, showers, boats sinking, alarms going off, and through them all was a constant thread of need, of release being denied.

Lee was sorely tempted to phone Joey and ask if he could come up for a little good morning love, but by the time he woke up, Joey would have already left for work. It didn't escape his notice as he jerked off in the shower that at least parts of his dreams were coming true. Just not the really good parts.

Revising his last two chapters took up Thursday, along with paperwork for the tree accident, and on Thursday evening he got an unexpected text message from Joey. Lee hadn't even realized his phone could text. Delighted, he replied to it, and they spent a couple of hours trading fast messages and flirting.

Friday night's movie date was looking more and more likely to be a date sans movie. Lee thought perhaps he should be resisting a little more, pressing for more of a "getting to know you" period, but his libido was all about getting a big hit of Joey.

Lee decided that maybe, for once, he'd follow his instinct instead of his better judgment. There wasn't a single thing about Joey that was setting off a warning or a voice or a signal in his animal brain. It felt right. It felt good.

Lee wanted it to feel even better.

He had an appointment with his advisor on Friday and it was all he could do to sit still through it and string his thoughts together into coherent sentences. He was sure that it was as plain as day that something was going on with him, but no one said anything to him: not the secretary for the department, not the assorted number of people he wound up talking to in the hallways, and not Dr. Young. It led Lee to believe that either the world at large was particularly unobservant or he usually walked around like a distracted, lust-addled undergrad. Both options were disturbing.

He had stopped thinking about it by the time he knocked on Joey's door and let himself in. By then he was thinking about whether he had to make small talk or whether it would be okay to rush Joey along to the bedroom or not.

The man himself was standing at the sink, running water from the tap into the filter pitcher. "Hey, you," he said with a smile. "Good day?"

"Pretty good." Lee went to him and kissed his mouth. "Getting better by the second. You?"

Joey turned off the water and left the pitcher in the sink, then turned in Lee's arms. "Same. I've got lasagna we can put in the oven later. Okay with you?"

"Uh-huh." Lee kissed him again, liking the way Joey fit against his body so easily. "Lasagna later."

Joey stretched against him like a cat, rubbing a little. "So, remember the other night?"

"It's hard to forget. There was a tree in the pool. There was a lack of coming, mere moments before my big finish." Which hadn't, in the end, stopped him from coming at all, just removed the active participation of Joey from the big moment.

"Yeah, that. I've been thinking about it a lot."

Lee smiled. "Have you? What have you been thinking?"

"That we waste a lot of time." With that, Joey kissed him again, slipped from his arms, and started pulling Lee through the house, clearly heading up to his room.

Laughing, Lee followed. "Not taking any chances, huh?"

"Not a one. I pulled back the covers, conveniently forgot to wear underwear, have the necessaries by the bed." Joey grinned at him as they climbed the stairs. "I even have an order of events."

"And people tell me I'm a control freak." Lee raised an eyebrow, but he was laughing still. "Tell me your plan."

They went down the short hall and by the time they were in the bedroom itself, they were both removing shirts and shoes. True to his word, Joey was commando and nicely stiff as he peeled off his jeans.

So was Lee.

"First," Joey said, not looking at Lee's face at all, "We get on the bed."

"I like it." Lee, naked, reached for Joey and had his hand swatted away. "I beg your pardon?"

Joey leered. "Lie down. Head on the pillows."

Lee, who had no real objection to lying naked on Joey's bed, did as he was told. His confusion melted away as Joey joined him, turning his body to nuzzle at Lee's balls, his own hips within easy reach of Lee's hands. "Oh, nice." Lee nodded, his legs parting to let Joey do whatever the hell he wanted. "Turn a bit."

When they were on their sides, Lee found the angle he liked best and set about melting Joey's brains through his dick. As expected, Lee liked all of Joey's flavors. He also discovered, incredibly quickly, that the magic of Joey's mouth didn't require being drunk or in a shower.

"Oh, Jesus Christ." Lee paused, his mouth against Joey's balls, and forced his spine to uncurl. "Save that for the end."

Joey chuckled, his mouth full of Lee's cock, and backed off.

"Thank you. God." Lee took a deep, steadying breath and went back to bathing Joey's balls, earning a deep moan. When he licked up the length of Joey's cock and ran his tongue over the head, Joey did the same to him and they both sighed. "Okay. Ready." Lee reached down and ran his fingers through Joey's hair, then opened wide to take Joey in.

They moved together for the first few strokes, long and slow sucks just to wet as much as they could. Lee sank his cock into Joey's mouth, pressed his tongue along Joey's prick, and followed his instinct. It felt amazing, warm and smooth, and with a soft noise he held onto Joey's hips and guided him in and out, let Joey fuck his mouth.

Head bobbing, Joey did the same, and very shortly they were both making sounds, hips shifting and tongues lapping wetly between sucks and pulls. Lee grunted when Joey pushed deep and his own cock throbbed; having the head of Joey's cock push the back of his throat was hot;

Joey did it again, his own sound vibrating in Lee's balls, and Lee nodded.

Joey pulled off Lee's cock, panting. "Oh, God." The words were mumbled against Lee's inner thigh, and he rocked his hips again. "Lee."

Lee tightened his fingers on Joey's hips and then let him go, let him move how he wanted to. Every thrust, every deep, hard stroke into his throat made Lee's balls ache. He wanted it as much as Joey did, and they both rolled slightly to give Joey better leverage.

"Next time," Joey said, panting. "Next time I'm going to watch your face." His hand dropped to the back of Lee's head, keeping him where Joey needed Lee to be. "Fuck. Honey."

Lee spread his legs wider and grabbed his cock while Joey fucked into him. His eyes were watering, his throat felt battered, but he was so hard he felt like his skin was going to split. Joey was groaning, his hips moving faster, and Lee could feel him getting bigger, swelling to spill. With a groan of his own, Lee used his other hand to pet Joey's balls, to mash them in his palm.

"Lee!" Joey came in a rush, his cock twitching wildly as he shot into Lee's throat. He eased off, still coming, and the taste spread over Lee's tongue.

Lee's hand flew on his cock, his balls hot and high, his eyes screwed closed as he chased his orgasm. He felt Joey move, sliding on him, panting against his skin, and then a finger pushed into Lee's ass and that was all he needed. He climaxed in a volley of come, long strands falling over his belly as Lee's body tightened up and released.

Neither of them spoke for a moment or two, and Lee wasn't even sure he could breathe.

"I think waiting would have been very, very wrong," Joey finally said, his voice serious. "We could have died."

"Obviously." Panting, his heart pounding in his chest, Lee reached for Joey and kissed him. "I think we should do it again after supper. Just to make sure we're okay."

"I think you're brilliant."

"You know, my advisor used that word today, too. But he wasn't talking sex. At least, I don't think so."

Joey laughed weakly. "You're in danger of being downgraded to merely 'bright' if you keep making bad jokes."

"I like you." Lee grinned and kissed him again.

"I like you, too." Joey looked at him, smiling. "I was serious about you spreading your work out in my guest room, you know. If you want to hang out with me while you study."

"You know what?" Lee had been thinking about that, in between sexual fantasies. "I think that when I'm hanging out with you, I want it to be about us. I can't work all the time. I shouldn't. I need to step back from it sometimes and just be me."

Joey beamed at him. "Okay."

"That does mean, however, that there's a good chance you might not see me for days at a time. And not be able to get rid of me for days at a time. It'll be up and down, and likely very inconvenient."

"Hey." Joey rolled over to face him. "I've been there, remember? I get it. Plus, you don't live very far away. If I start to pine, I'll merely bring you down a plate of food and give you a kiss."

Lee smiled. "You have no idea how great that sounds."

"It sounds pretty great to me, too."

Lee kissed him. There was come getting sticky on his chest. "I'm kind of neurotic." He whispered it as if he were in a confessional. "You should know that, too. And I have issues about status and money and my lack of both."

Joey snorted. "I've been told."

"I knew I shouldn't have given your number to Tony."

"He adores you, you know." Joey was still smiling at him.

"He's a little crazy."

"Stop that." Joey kissed him. "Let's shower. Then I'll feed you. Then we can come back here and discover all kinds of things about each other."

Lee nodded and took Joey's hand. "I'll try not to be too neurotic."

"And I'll try not to be too enthusiastic."

Laughing, Lee let Joey take him to the shower, protesting the whole way about how much he liked Joey's enthusiasm.

Chapter Twelve
The Call

Lasagna, they discovered, wasn't a food meant to be eaten in bed.

Once they'd finished eating, stripped the bed and put the sheets in the wash—liberally doused in stain remover—and made the bed up again with a second set of sheets, Joey offered Lee his choice of movies.

"Are we actually going to watch a movie," Lee asked thoughtfully, "or am I merely selecting the background noise?" Since they were both naked again he was reasonably sure he knew the answer to that.

Joey grinned and fanned the DVD cases out. "You tell me."

One eyebrow up, Lee reached out and selected one of the *Lord of the Rings* movies. He didn't care which one; he knew the story well enough to start paying attention at any point and all three films were incredibly long. The chances of being distracted by the menu screen when the movie ended were slim to none; they'd probably be asleep by that point.

Without comment, Joey put the movie in the player and joined Lee on the bed. It was a big bed, and while it was completely possible that they could both sprawl comfortably and not even touch each other, they both gravitated to the middle, dragging pillows with them to make a nest.

Lee was nuzzling into Joey's neck before the navigation menu was even on the screen, and Joey laughed, trying to start the movie while being distracted. Lee still had no idea which movie it was, and he didn't care.

"You're focused," Joey pointed out, finally tossing the remote to the end of the bed, the movie starting. "This is not a complaint."

"Good." Lee kissed him, moving as close to Joey as he could get without being inside him, though that was the ultimate goal. Joey seemed to be right there with him, pliant and malleable when Lee started arranging their limbs.

"Did you... can you reach the..." Joey's sentences couldn't seem to find their endings as Lee draped one of Joey's legs over his own thighs and started petting Joey's balls.

"Got it all." Lee kissed him, licking through Joey's mouth and silencing him for the moment by simply not letting him talk. He rolled Joey's balls and stroked his inner thighs, occasionally hefted Joey's cock and played with it for a few moments. For his part, Joey didn't seem to know if he wanted to hang on tight to Lee's arms or if he wanted to bury his hands in Lee's hair and direct the kisses.

Lee let him do both. He was content to kiss and touch for long minutes; they didn't have to rush. Everything they'd done had been such a rush, from their first drunken groping to the way they'd hurried upstairs to make sure they had time for even simple oral sex.

Not that he wanted this to be slow and sweet lovemaking. Not by a long shot; Lee wanted as intense as

Joey was willing to go. But he didn't think that they had to hurry to get there.

"Lee." Joey kissed him and kissed him again, but with a low moan as Lee's fingers trailed over soft skin. "Please."

"Please?" Lee grinned and rubbed at Joey's perineum. "This, please?"

"Yeah. More, please." Joey's hips moved back and forth, and his cock bumped nicely at Lee's forearm. "Touch me."

Lee pulled his hand away and licked two fingers, then rubbed with them, slippery and wet for a few moments. "Not enough, huh?" He traced Joey's hole and held on tight when Joey jerked in his arms and his body tried to open right away. "Oh, man."

Joey nodded, starting to breathe more heavily. "Want. A lot."

"I can tell." Lee reached for the lube. "Are you going to be able to stand some play, or do you want to just do it?"

Joey flushed and buried his face in Lee's neck while Lee opened the lube. "You can... if you want. You can play with my ass for a while. If I come, you can fuck me anyway."

Lee nodded, his breath catching. "Will you? Come, I mean."

"Probably." Joey shifted restlessly and Lee could feel the first smears on his arm as Joey's cock started to leak.

Lee rubbed lube between his fingers and made sure the container was closed before he let go of it. "Total bottom?" he asked, dropping his hand down to Joey's ass again. "Just for information's sake."

"Not always, no. For now, yes." Joey mouthed Lee's neck and moaned. "But this is a lot more fun with another person."

Lee froze for a moment, then the mental images kicked in and he grinned. "You dirty boy."

"Shut up. If you want, you can watch. Sometime. Not now."

Lee huffed a laugh and nodded. "Yeah. I'll watch." He traced around Joey's ass again and pushed two fingers in, nice and slow. "But I'm busy now."

Joey groaned, his teeth worrying at Lee's skin. "Busy," he agreed. He flexed and his body gripped Lee's fingers tightly. "Get busy."

Still chuckling, Lee moved his head back so he could watch Joey's face and started to finger-fuck him. Slow and deep, fast and shallow, Joey seemed to like it all. He was panting within moments, trying to move his hips to match Lee's rhythm, but he couldn't quite catch it. Frustrated, he growled and lay back.

"That's it." Lee nodded and let Joey lie down on the bed, his legs spread and his feet flat on the mattress. "You do what you need to do." He pushed another finger in, squirted lube in the general area, and went to work on Joey's balls and cock with the other hand. His own erection was all but forgotten as Joey started to come apart at the seams.

Joey's hands fisted in the sheets and his hips lifted and fell. Sounds spilled from his mouth as Lee played with him, but Joey's eyes were staring, sightlessly, at the ceiling.

"That's it," Lee crooned again. He was jacking Joey's cock faster, tighter, and the fingers in Joey's ass were pressing and stroking, making Joey shudder and swear. "Come if you want to. I want to see it. I want to fuck you when you get your breath back; I can wait. You'll still be wet, open. I'll just slide right in. You can sit on my lap and—"

Joey arched off the bed and came, his cock throbbing

as he shot.

"Nice." Lee stroked him through it, felt Joey's ass clenching and releasing around his fingers. "So pretty." He was. He was stunningly pretty, flushed skin and wild, dark hair.

"Fuck me," Joey panted at him. "Don't wait. Get in me. Now. Please."

Lee raised an eye brow and kept stroking him, far more gently than before. "Are you sure?"

"Do you see me getting soft?" Joey let go of the bed sheets and reached for Lee's wrist, dragging Lee's hand away from his ass. "Get your cock in my ass. Now."

Lee blinked and made a mad scramble for the condoms, getting one on in record time. Even then it took more than a few seconds, time in which Joey had pounced, pushed, and straddled.

"Aim," Joey demanded. There were streaks of come on his belly.

Lee looked up at him, held his cock at the right angle and guided Joey down onto him, all without breathing. "Oh, my holy fuck." Joey was hot and wet and he could move.

"Yes!" Joey braced himself by putting his hands flat on Lee's chest and started rocking, lifting himself up and dropping down, fast. He was just as frantic as he'd been before he'd come and Lee could only follow along.

Feet planted, Lee slammed up to meet him and was rewarded with another curse, a flex of Joey's ass, and an even faster response. "God," Lee whispered. "I don't know if I want you to switch."

Joey grinned at him and wiggled and lights went off behind Lee's eyes.

"Joey." It was supposed to be a warning to knock that kind of thing off, but Joey did it again and Lee felt his own cock throb and swell. "Joey."

Groaning, Joey leaned back, reaching. The angle made him get impossibly tight and Lee knew, just knew that Joey was going to blow again. "Ready?" Joey asked him.

"For what?" It was a stupid question, but Lee asked anyway. Then he yelled as Joey's finger slid into Lee's ass and they both moved in a hard jolt, coming at the same time.

It was like nothing Lee had felt before. His cock was throbbing and his balls were pulsing, and all around him Joey was going at a different rhythm. It was incredible and intense, and possibly the very best first time sex anyone had ever had with any partner, ever.

Lee was nothing if not sure that no one else ever felt as good as he did.

"I am never getting out of bed with you," he slurred as Joey curled up, both on and next to him, both of them panting for air.

"I still want to get a hold of you after you're done mowing the lawn, though." Joey leered at him, which looked a little out of place on a face that was so flushed from recent orgasm. Lee could still feel the hard thump of Joey's heartbeat under his hand. "So, so sexy. You can't even know how many times I've jerked off thinking about you, all sweaty and smelling of fresh grass."

Lee shook his head. "You're very good at hiding your lust, man. I had no clue you were even watching. You could have flirted a little, you know."

Joey blushed and shrugged. Lee hadn't thought that Joey's cheeks could go any pinker. "You were always so distracted and serious. I thought maybe you were straight, or in a relationship, or that you didn't like people."

Lee winced. "I think a lot about my dissertation when I'm doing yard work. It makes me look like a snob, huh?"

Joey kissed him. "Maybe. But it's still hot as hell. And I know now that you're definitely approachable."

"That's one way to put it," Lee said with a laugh. "Also, insatiable."

"Dude. I can't go again. Not without a nap."

"So nap." Lee grinned and took only the minimum amount of time to finally dispose of the rubber before he snuggled in, fully intent on getting enough rest to go one more round before he had to return to academics and yard work.

Still. It gave him something to plan around; Lee had a feeling that he was riding a little momentum in terms of his dissertation. If he was going to be working a lot, it might be an idea to give Joey a bit of a treat when he had a break. He fell asleep, smiling and sticky, planning when he could next mow the lawn.

As it turned out, he had to get it mowed on a day Joey was working late, so for a week and a half the two of them continued on as usual, phoning, visiting and sending text messages. Joey tried to take Lee to a play one night, but Lee sat down and explained that dinner and theater dates would underline the economic imbalance in their relationship and that he wasn't comfortable with that. Joey told him he was slightly ridiculous but highly adorable, and then they had fast and athletic blow jobs in Lee's living room, so that worked out okay.

Lee was mired in the third to last chapter of his dissertation the next time the lawn required mowing, and because of his distraction, had forgotten his grand plan for seduction. He walked and pushed the mower, the vibrations making his hands tingle and the sun making his back hot. He knew that the whole of the yard took him only about forty-five minutes; hopefully he could find a way to word his deconstruction of the particular theory in such a way that he wouldn't actually use the word "stupid" in his first draft.

He paused halfway through the lawn to dump the bag of clippings into the composter by the very back wall, and took his time reattaching it. Perhaps if he pulled a sentence or two from the introductory chapter, he could start wrapping up the section.

A low whistle made him look up, though he wasn't sure where it came from. The sun was too bright, and it probably wasn't meant for him, anyway. He got the bag attached and zipped it up, then stood up, covered in clippings and more than a few smudges of dirt.

"Hey!"

Lee's head snapped up. He shaded his eyes and looked toward Joey's deck. "Oh. You're home," he called. "How are you doing?"

"Could not possibly be better. You're going to come and see me the instant you finish the yard, right?"

Lee immediately looked over at Stephanie's deck, but it was blessedly empty.

"Relax," Joey said, laughing. "There's no one around. I took the afternoon off."

Lee looked around at the yard. "You ruined my concentration, you know." He didn't actually mind. "Maybe I should take a break now."

"I think not." Joey waved a finger at him. "You do your work. I'll watch."

So Lee mowed the lawn with an ever-increasing sense of unreality. He'd been perfectly willing to do this on his terms and in his time; he'd even thought that it would be kind of fun to look up at the end of mowing the lawn to see Joey watching and wanting him. This knowing, though, and being watched... It made him move faster, if nothing else. He was turned on, he was vaguely uncomfortable, and he was also embarrassed. Being the object of someone's lust was all well and good behind closed doors. Knowing that Joey was looking at him and anticipating merely made Lee feel an odd sense of pressure to live up to the image of being precisely what he didn't want to be. The maintenance man. Role play without the play.

Still. He got hard, he couldn't think about politics, and he was pretty sure they were about to christen Joey's kitchen counter. Lee could handle that.

With the lawn done he looked up at Joey's deck. "Five minutes. I need to clean the mower and dump the clippings." He casually adjusted his cock in his shorts and hoped to God that none of the other tenants were watching.

"I'll unlock the kitchen door."

Lee grinned and took off, taking the mower down to the shed to clean it up. He worked fast, but made sure he did an okay job of it; he got all the stuff off the blades and scraped out from under the deck, anyway. Once it was locked safely in the shed, he headed for Joey's.

He didn't run, or even jog, though it was mostly the state of his dick that dictated his pace.

The kitchen door was unlocked as he went in, and he lifted the edge of his shirt to wipe his face. "I need a glass of water," he said, smiling at the way Joey was staring at him. "Okay?"

Joey nodded. He was wearing a T-shirt, too, and cargo shorts, and he looked about ready to eat Lee alive. He got Lee a bottle of water from the fridge and moved close enough to undo Lee's shorts. "You just drink that. Lean on the counter. I'll take care of this."

Lee laughed and nodded. "Go for it." Like he'd turn that action down.

Joey got Lee's zipper lowered and was just reaching inside when the phone rang. "Ignore it."

Lee ignored it, gasping as Joey's hand found what

it was looking for. "Okay. How many rings until the machine?"

The phone rang again and Joey lifted Lee's cock out, holding its weight in his palm. "One more. Then I'll suck you off."

Lee drank water fast, his hips rocking. He moaned as Joey stroked him, Joey's thumb rubbing at the head. The phone rang again and Joey went to his knees.

"You've reached Doctor Joey Reed. I can't take your call right now, please leave a message."

Dr. Joey Reed had a mouthful of cock and Lee was looking down, watching as he pushed in, nice and slow. "Nice. So nice."

"Joey, it's Ira. Call me, please, honey." There was a pause and both Joey and Lee froze. Ira's tone of voice was enough to kill any intentions they had. He took a breath and said, "TCF phone tree, if we can do it. I've got bad news."

Lee pulled out of Joey's mouth without thinking about it and Joey got back to his feet, both of them turning to look at the phone mounted on the wall.

"Ken Hayes is dead." Ira's voice paused again, heavy with sadness. "He committed suicide."

Chapter Thirteen
The Things We Don't Say

Joey went to the phone and picked it up, leaving Lee to lean on the counter as he tried to remember how to breathe. It felt like all the air in the room, in the house, in the world had been sucked away, leaving him to go numb and cold.

"Ira, I'm here." Joey sounded calm, his voice liquid smooth. "I was busy, sorry. Do you have any details?"

Details. Lee blinked slowly and did his shorts back up, noting absently that his dick was wet with spit. It didn't matter; his whole body was cold, sweat drying in the air conditioning. Joey would get details, find out where and when, and if there was a place they could go. There should be; Ken was based on the east coast, had helped to design buildings in cities that were within a day or two's drive. He'd even designed a dorm at Legacy, now that Lee thought of it, and had been one of the designers for the new chapel at CSUC. Joey would find out.

"I can call Echo," Joey was saying. "And Lee's here, he has numbers for a guy in his year and Tony Sanchez for sure. His Junior, too. Lee?"

Lee looked at him and nodded hazily. "Yeah. Yeah, I

can call Tony and René. Matt. Maybe a couple of others. Matt was the social one."

Joey peered at him. "Are you okay?"

Lee shook his head, then nodded. "Yeah, I'm fine."

"Ira, I have to go." Joey turned to look at the wall, one hand rubbing at his hair. "I'll call you in an hour or so, okay?"

Lee blinked again and realized Joey was hanging up because Lee was freaking out. With an effort he pulled himself up, literally, and tried to force his mind to focus. He would call Tony, then Matt. René, when he knew a little better what was going on. They'd get the word out, and those who could come, would.

"Yeah, I got it. Day after tomorrow, three o'clock. I'll call Echo. Oh, and Darren. Talk soon." Joey hung up and turned to face him again. Lee must have done an okay job of taming his expression, because Joey lost a little of the wariness he'd had, a little of the fright. "Okay?"

"Yeah." Lee nodded. "Sorry. A bit of a shock." He patted his pockets until he found his cell. "Day after tomorrow?" he prompted.

Joey nodded and came to him, sliding into his arms and hugging him hard. "Yes. The service is at three, at the CSUC chapel."

Lee hugged him back. "Okay." He didn't ask if he knew how Ken had died. He didn't think he could bear to know how, or why. Not while his brain was still half asleep. "I'll phone Tony." The question slipped out, his tongue at war with his will. "How did he...?"

"Ira says he hanged himself." Joey whispered. "I'll call Echo. He's closest."

Absurdly, Lee wanted to tell him to say hi from him. Instead, he blotted out the mental image of a man hanging from a rope and scrolled through his phone book. He called Tony, walking through to the dining room while the call connected. Joey was already using his landline, pacing the kitchen.

The phone rang twice and Peter answered. "Hello, Lee," he said quietly. "Tony's using his cell to make calls. You're on his list."

Lee nodded. "Uh-huh. How did he hear?"

Peter sighed. "It was on the news. Then the phone rang. He's talking to Nassim at the moment; hang on."

"Sure."

There was a long pause and Tony's voice came. "Are you okay?"

"I'm... at the moment. Yes. Do you know about the service?" Lee looked at the prints on the dining room wall and then moved to the china cabinet to study the photographs behind the glass.

"Yeah. I'll be there." Tony sounded firm. "Nassim can't, though. Are you coming up?"

Lee nodded. "Yeah. Tomorrow, probably."

"I'll take an early flight, stay that night. I'll find you."

"Good. I'll need you."

"I'm sorry, Lee. I know he helped you when you needed it."

"I'm sorry I didn't get the chance to do the same." Lee blinked rapidly as his eyes stung. "I need to call Matt and René."

"See you soon," Tony said softly and hung up.

From the kitchen came Joey's voice, muted by the door, and Lee took a moment to re-compose himself before he called Matt. This would be harder; Matt and Ken had been fairly friendly, the three of them taking over the pool table together more often than not.

"Hello?"

Lee looked at Joey's photos again and tried to figure out who were family and who were friends. "Hi, is Matt home?"

"In the garage. Hang on." It wasn't the same person who had answered the first time he'd called, Lee thought. At least, there was no joking, no yelling. Just a door opening and closing and then Matt's voice, saying hello.

"Matt, hey. It's Scout."

"Jesus, you sound like shit. Don't tell me you and Joey are having trouble already."

"No." Lee smiled a little and then winced. "Jem, I've got some bad news for you."

There was a long pause and then Matt asked, "How bad? Should I be sitting?"

"Yeah, maybe."

"Christ." Matt took a deep, loud breath. "If someone ain't dead I'm gonna have your ass for scaring—"

"Ken. Ken's dead." He blurted it, not able to handle Matt's nervous chatter, not right then and not that way. "He. He's dead."

The silence stretched between them for so long that Lee had to breathe. He couldn't hold his breath that long, and Matt wasn't saying anything. "Matt?"

"I'm here." He sounded like Lee felt, hollow and fragile. "What happened?"

"I'm not sure." Lee whispered, as if not saying it out loud would make it not true. "He... Ira, Joey's Senior called. He said it was suicide. Tony found out on the news, he's been calling people. There's... there's going to be a service day after tomorrow at the CSUC chapel. Three o'clock."

"Shut up." Matt was whispering, too. "Suicide? Ken?"

Lee swallowed, hard. "Matt. Can you. Will you?"

"Yeah. Yeah, of course. Hang on, I'm going inside. I'll get online and book a room at the Dunkirk. When are you going to get there?"

"I don't know." Lee pulled out one of the dining

room chairs and sat down. He couldn't hear Joey talking anymore. "I'll have to call my advisor, and the complex management, give them the heads up. I'd like to go tomorrow, but it'll depend on if I can get a pool service to check in here or not. The rest should be okay for a couple of days."

"Okay." He could hear Matt walking. "I'll go up tomorrow anyway; there'll be a lot of people coming in. Ken was a big name, you know? Up and coming, won some awards."

Lee nodded and traced the line of the table leaf in front of him. "Yeah. Lots of people." He wondered if his dinner jacket would be okay to wear. He hadn't been planning to buy a proper suit until his dissertation defense.

Joey came in, moving slowly, and sat down across from him.

"Want me to book a double?" Matt offered. "You can room with me. It'll be like old times, but without the booze and homework."

Lee tried to smile but couldn't quite do it. "Thanks, but no. I'll come up with Joey. We'll figure something out."

"I'm not going."

Lee looked at Joey, confused. "What do you mean you're not going? You can get time off work, I'm sure." He wasn't sure, truthfully, but the idea of anyone saying that Joey couldn't go to a funeral didn't really fall into the realm of possibility, as far as Lee was concerned.

In his ear, Matt said nothing at all.

"I can get time," Joey agreed with a nod. "But I won't. I'm not going. If you'd like, you can take my car, though."

"But, why?"

"Hey, Scout? I'll book the double. If you don't bunk with me, it's cool. Love you."

"Love you, too," Lee said absently. "I'll call you in the morning."

"Sure thing. Don't fight. Okay? Do not fight. Not when you're both messed up." Matt hung up before Lee could tell him that they weren't going to fight, that there wasn't anything to fight about.

"Why aren't you coming to Ken's funeral?" he asked, looking at Joey and trying to read his face. It wasn't easy; Joey had gone utterly blank on him, and was looking pale and tired more than anything else.

"It's a memorial service, not a full funeral. And I can't. That's all. Echo will be there; Ira can't make it. Is Tony going?"

Lee nodded slowly. "Yeah. Tony, Matt. Me. I need to call René. Why won't you tell me?"

Joey looked away and lifted one shoulder a little. "I... I don't deal very well with things like this. I can't go. I'm sorry. It's just that I choose not to go to funerals and events like them; I don't grieve in public very well. I seem to get even more upset than I normally would and I don't find them to be any kind of closure. I've learned how to say good by on my own, is all. I'm sorry, Lee."

Lee stood up, feeling immeasurably older than he had ten minutes before. "It's okay." It wasn't really, but Lee knew it was the wrong time to be selfish about needing Joey by his side. Everyone dealt with things in their own way. "I need to go and pack, make some phone calls. I'll call you tonight."

"Okay." Joey stayed where he was, his face sad and gray. "Please do. I meant it about my car."

Lee shook his head. "I'll take the bus. You might change your mind and need it." He left via the kitchen and had reached his cottage before he realized he hadn't kissed Joey goodbye.

Chapter Fourteen
There and Back Again

When Lee got the phone call that his grandmother had passed away, alone in her kitchen, he packed his bag and walked to the bus station, not even sure how much a ticket cost. He found out he had enough in his pocket, barely, but that he'd missed the bus by half an hour and the next one wouldn't leave for another seven hours.

Not wanting to spend seven hours in the bus station trying not to cry, trying not to panic, he went to the only place he could think of, despite it being the middle of the morning in the middle of the week. At least he would be alone at the house and he could cry if he needed to, without housemates around to speculate on the state of his romantic life.

It was raining and cold, but inside the house he felt cocooned. The gray sky and the rivulets of water running on the huge glass windows were suited to the mood, to the bleakness of the day, and Lee stood there, all alone, and watched the rain come down. He didn't even notice that his cheeks were wet with tears until he had to wipe his nose, and then he couldn't seem to stop. He felt like he was going to be sick from trying to keep his grief inside, from letting it out. The sounds of it were harsh in his throat, and harder on his ears, but still he couldn't stop.

Arms, strong and warm, came around him, holding him fiercely. "What happened? Lee. Tell me where you're hurt."

Lee fell into Ken's arms and suddenly couldn't stand under his own power. "She's dead," he sobbed. "Gram. She's all I have left and she's dead and I wasn't there."

"Oh." It was a sigh, breathed into his ear, understanding and sympathy all together. "Oh, Lee. I'm so sorry."

Ken held him and comforted him, petting Lee's hair and not saying anything at all. He didn't tell Lee it was going to be okay—it wasn't. He didn't say that he was there for Lee—he clearly was. All Ken Hayes did was let Lee cry and hold him close. When Lee stopped crying, exhausted and weak, Ken didn't let go. "I'm sorry," he said again. "I'll help you."

"How?" Lee was numb and sure that there wasn't anything Ken could do—anyone could do—that would help.

"I'll go see your department head. Tell them you've had to go home for a while and why. Then you can call the office when you're not quite so messed up."

Lee hadn't even thought of that. "Okay," he whispered. He was still leaning into Ken, aware that they'd moved to the couch, but not sure when. "Thank you."

"Do you have anyone?" Ken asked. "When you get home, is there anyone there for you?"

Lee shook his head and another few tears slipped out. "No. Just me." No aunts or uncles, no cousins. He would have to tell the neighbors and call Miss Marthy, Gram's best friend. No, that wasn't right. Lee blinked slowly. Miss Marthy had called him and started crying, then a man had taken the phone. The police officer who'd done the wellness check when Gram didn't answer the phone.

Miss Marthy knew. "Just me," he said again.

"I'll go with you."

Lee shook his head. "Ken. You can't just take off with me for a few days, go to a place you've never been like this."

Ken helped Lee sit up and put their foreheads together. "You need to plan a funeral. You need to bury your last blood relative. I'm going with you."

Lee started to cry again. Relief and love tasted the same as grief, and it hurt just as much as it tore out of his body, but Ken was right there, holding him up.

The bus smelled the same, though the colors of the seat coverings had changed. Maybe it was a different bus line; Lee couldn't be sure. It felt the same, only this time he was riding alone.

It wasn't raining, but it was gray and foggy, and the glass felt cool on his forehead as he leaned to look behind them. The road hadn't been particularly familiar to him, and he'd spent the whole trip trying to avoid thinking anyway, so his mind felt as foggy as the air.

He'd called Joey after he'd packed, but still had no idea why Joey wouldn't come. Unable to understand, hurting in his heart for multiple reasons ranging from grief to confusion, Lee had finally told Joey that he would miss him and hung up.

He didn't sleep very well.

Matt had called his cell around lunch time to make sure Lee was still going, and Lee had apologized for not calling him like he'd promised. So many little things were slipping through his fingers; he'd called his boss, called the pool company, but had once again forgotten to tell the school. A long distance call plus roaming fees later, he'd taken care of that, and all that was left to do was read or look out the window and think.

He read.

Darkness had fallen by the time the bus got to the station, and it was well after nine p.m. when he checked in at the Dunkirk. Matt had gotten a double as promised, and left a message for him at the desk.

Drop your bag in the room, grab a shower, meet me in the hotel bar. Jem.

It sounded like the perfect plan to Lee. He hoped there would be about a hundred people crowded into a space built for fifty, so he could sit in the corner and try to blend in with the wallpaper. Matt would let him do that, since he'd have an open shot at making Lee talk later, back in their room.

Lee took his keycard from the desk clerk and went to the room, his shoes making no sound at all on the thick carpeting; the Dunkirk had remodeled and Lee was grateful he and Matt were sharing a room. He wasn't sure if he could afford it on his own, not now that it was "well appointed" instead of merely "quaint."

The rooms had been given a facelift, too, since the last time he'd been to town. That had been the fall after he'd graduated when he'd come back for homecoming to see René, who was now too far west to make it back for the memorial. Since he had never met Ken, it wasn't a surprise at all, and he'd been sincere in his condolences. He'd lost a brother, too, if only in an abstract sense, and said that he'd look up Ken's obituary online and make an appropriate memorial.

Morose, travel weary, and wishing he was better able to process these situations, Lee let himself into the hotel room. He looked around and put his bag on the bed that was clearly not Matt's, then he realized he was smiling. Matt, his Matt, his Jem, hadn't changed very much if the state of the room was anything to go by.

Clothes, books, two ball caps, and a bag of potato chips were spread out over one of the beds, and an empty duffle bag was in the middle of the floor. The rest of the room was pristine, as if a mini-cyclone had whirled through the room and left again, leaving isolated damage.

With a shake of his head Lee pulled clean jeans and a long sleeved T-shirt out of his bag and went to shower. He smelled like the bus, and that was not to be lingered upon any more than necessary, or tolerated. The bathroom had been missed by cyclone Matt, so Lee didn't have to deal with wet towels or anything more dangerous than his own distraction.

When he went looking for the bar he took his lapel pin with him, unsure how to wear it on his shirt but unwilling to leave it in the room. It just seemed like the thing to do. He had his wallet, his cell phone, his room key; everything else was waiting for him downstairs.

Or was back home, without him.

Lee checked his phone as he went down in the elevator, but there weren't any text messages waiting for him. He sent one to Joey, to let him know that he'd arrived, and crossed the lobby to the open doors of the bar, following the sounds of a piano and the murmur of voices.

He'd expected to see a few tables of people, all of them obviously his people; a part of him had hoped for it, needed it. Instead there was a table of four women, a cluster of men huddled around a laptop, clearly working while they had a beer or two, and a man at the bar, reading a newspaper. Matt was nowhere to be seen.

With a sigh Lee walked up to the bar and sat down. He'd order a beer and wait for Matt to come back from the bathroom or wherever he'd gone—maybe outside if he'd started smoking cigars again, although Lee hoped not. Cell phone on the top of the bar, Lee looked around as he waited for the bartender to make his way to him.

The place seemed nice enough, and aside from an upgrade to the decor, it appeared the same as it had always been. "Some things never change," he murmured to himself. Unlike the rooms, he was pretty sure the prints on the walls hadn't been changed out at all, and the photos were the same, without doubt.

"Scout."

Lee looked toward the door, fast, and caught Matt in a flying hug. "There you are." He didn't let go, just held on tight. Matt felt good against him, real. Dressed in jeans and a T-shirt with a CSUC hoodie over it, Matt even looked the same as he had three years ago. His curls might have been a little shorter under the ever-present ball cap. "Missed you."

Matt hugged him back. "How are you holding up?"

"I've been better." Lee finally pulled back and let him go, just as the bartender arrived. "What are you drinking?"

"Jack." Matt sat down, pulling out his own cell phone and putting it on the bar.

Lee ordered two and a beer, then sat next to him. "Have you talked to anyone else?"

"Yeah." Matt fished a piece of paper out of his back pocket. "I called our year, they can't come, and a couple from the year ahead of us who can. I feel like I've been on the phone forever. Leon called me right after you did—Tony had called him. Their whole year is coming. He rattled off a bunch of names that I didn't even recognize, guys from before our time. And then I called my Junior, Kirk."

Lee nodded, overwhelmed. "Did you get any sleep last night?"

"No." Matt nodded his thanks to the bartender and both he and Lee handed over their credit cards, opening tabs. "But that's okay. I'll sleep tonight."

"What did Kirk say?" Lee had scattered memories of a slight, dark haired young guy with a very serious disposition. He was pretty much the exact opposite of the personality he'd expected Matt to choose for his Junior, but Matt adored him.

"That he'd come up from Florida and call everyone he could think of." Matt gave Lee a long look with sharp eyes. "And he asked me to pass his condolences on to you, specifically."

Lee stared and then looked away. "Why me?" He hunched over the bar, drinking his beer. His pin jabbed him in the hip and he took it out of his pocket. "Where's yours?"

Matt pointed to his hat. "Here, let me." He took Lee's and pinned it to Lee's shirt cuff, just above his wrist watch. "There you go. And because what Ken did for you when your Gram passed is to that year what Cesar and Phil were to ours. Brothers having each other's back."

Tearing up again, Lee nodded and looked at his drinks. "I'm so mad at him," he whispered. "I would have helped."

Matt's arm slid across his shoulders. "I know, man. I do." He kissed Lee's cheek. "We all would have."

Lee sighed and nodded, leaning into Matt.

"Mmm." Matt touched his phone, spinning it a little. "Echo's coming, by the way. Tomorrow. Most everyone I talked to is arriving tomorrow and staying the one night."

"I really needed to be here." Lee leaned a little more, then sat up again. "I'm glad you came."

"I needed it, too." Matt finished his drink and waved at the bartender. "Drink up. There's a guy going to sit at the piano. Let's sing badly and toast our brothers. Who knows, some more might show up."

"That'd be cool." He looked around the nearly empty bar. "This place needs Family."

The man at the piano started playing a melody that sounded vaguely familiar and Lee drank his drink. When he realized he was staring at his phone, willing it to give him a text message from Joey, he shoved it in his pocket and ordered another drink. "Come on. Let's go sit at the piano."

Matt went with him, and for a while they just sat and talked about whatever came to mind, including Lee's dissertation, Matt's lack of boyfriend, and what the hell the waiter was thinking, wearing a shirt that color with the bar's uniform tie. That last comment from Matt had made the pianist smile, and Lee finally requested a song. "Can you play Big Spender for my bitchy friend here? He'll even sing."

"I so will not." But Matt did, belting it out just like the song was meant to be sung. Matt had a surprisingly good voice, really, and as he didn't bother changing any of the pronouns, Lee had a great time watching him. After that, the piano saw a lot more attention as Matt kept going, picking out songs as Lee ordered drinks. Hey, Look Me Over was followed by If My Friends Could See Me Now, and for the first time in what felt like days, Lee was smiling.

It had only been a day, he reminded himself.

Matt, drinking water so Lee wouldn't have to carry him upstairs, was discussing the merits of picking a song from a later decade with one of the women who'd come farther into the bar to catch his act, and Lee, distracted by his returning sadness, turned to the man at the piano to suggest he play what he was in the mood for before Matt could take over. "Unless you want to spend the evening playing power ballads from the eighties, 'cause that's where he's headed next."

That got a smile. "I think I know a few of those."

"What are you drinking?" Lee asked, pulling in the roaming waiter with the bad shirt choice.

After determining that the bar didn't have a single wine from Australia, the pianist ordered a Bud Light Lime and thanked Lee for it. Then his eyes narrowed and looked hard at Lee, then at Matt. "I think we have something in common," he said softly, his southern accent somehow more pronounced. "My lapel pin is upstairs, on my lapel, oddly enough. Carrigan Chantz, class of '91." He held out his right hand.

Delighted, shocked, Lee grinned and noted the missing thumb. "I know." He shook Carrigan's hand. "Lee Sutton, class of '02. So is Frank Sinatra, over there. He's a fan of yours."

Carrigan eyed Matt with appreciation. "I might be a fan of his. Or would be, if we weren't in town for this particular reason."

"He's easy to like." Lee leaned over and tugged at Matt's sleeve. "Hey, Frank. Come meet family."

Matt turned, instantly dismissing the woman he'd been talking to. "Pardon?"

"Matt Lewis, Carrigan Chantz." Lee snorted as Matt did a classic double take and then went suddenly red. "And here it comes."

"Jesus fucking Christ, are you kidding me!?"

Lee rolled his eyes. "Matthew. Indoor voice, public space, solemn occasion."

Matt waved him off, already shaking Carrigan's hand. "Lee told me you were a brother, years ago, but I didn't believe him. Well, I looked in the book and then I did, but I was sure someone was making it up. Wow. Carrigan Chantz." He sat down right on the piano bench next to him. "I'm Matt."

Carrigan laughed, apparently delighted. "Hello, Matt.

It's nice to meet you."

They ordered another round of drinks, the women left, and Matt asked Carrigan if he'd ever met Ken.

"Twice." Carrigan nodded as the three of them moved to a table. "Both times were at events; the first time was a classic near miss. He moved away from the bar, I dodged right, he went the same way and his drink wound up splashing me. He was wiping it away, full of apologies, when he saw my pin."

Lee smiled a little. "Those pins. Gotta love 'em."

Matt rolled his eyes. "I've never met anyone with mine." He might have been pouting.

Carrigan looked like he thought Matt pouting was adorable, but he turned his attention to Lee. "You have?"

Lee nodded and opened his mouth, but Matt jumped in.

"His boyfriend," Matt said, reaching for Lee's beer. "He met his boyfriend that way."

Lee lifted a shoulder. He supposed Joey was his boyfriend, after all. "Joey Reed," he supplied. "Class of '97. His Senior was Ira... oh, crap. I've forgotten Ira's last name."

"Kline. Ira Kline. Hell of a guy." Carrigan nodded. "He isn't able to come, I don't think."

"I know." Lee nodded. "Matt's got a list of people he's talked to. Did you talk to Ira?" He felt like he was grasping at straws, trying to find out what was up with Joey.

Carrigan shook his head. "You actually met a brother by pin, to turn a phrase, and now you're dating him?"

Lee nodded and filled in the blanks, leaving out anything that wasn't important. Swimming wasn't even mentioned.

"But he's not here." Carrigan leaned back, apparently

mulling that over.

"Nope." Lee sighed. "He's not. I wish he was, but he couldn't make it."

"He might show up tomorrow," Matt said sympathetically.

Lee nodded and let it go. There were songs to sing and toasts to make, and he'd just met another brother. He had Matt, he had TCF. At home, he had Joey.

But he didn't have Ken anymore, and that was what he needed to focus on.

Glass in the air, immediately met by Carrigan's and Matt's, he said, "To our brother Ken. May he have the love of his Family, always."

"To Ken."

Chapter Fifteen
Goodbye, Brother

Going to a memorial feeling slightly hung over was not something Lee wanted to experience. He and Matt stayed up half the night talking, and at one point there were tears. There were also whispered confessions about deep feelings regarding growing up and getting real lives, and there was far too much sharing of sex stories, but by the time Lee went to sleep he was no longer drunk and he knew he could face the day without wincing.

Three in the afternoon was a long way off from breakfast. Matt and Lee drove around for a while, seeing the town and what had changed, cruising through campus and past the house where Lee had roomed. They didn't go to the house of The Chosen Family; that was the domain of the current members. Lee had his key back on his key ring, though, and he'd bet money that Matt did as well.

Lee tried to reach Joey four times, getting no answer at his house, on his cell, at the lab. He'd never called there before and felt very odd doing it; he didn't try that number again.

His text messages remained unanswered.

"Maybe he's on his way," Matt said, holding his hand as they arrived back at the hotel. "Hey. It'll be okay."

Lee nodded. "Yeah," he said softly. "It'll work out. I've got my own issues I'm bringing to this, I know. I hate that I can't reach him, though. I just want to say hi, see if he's okay. He was sad, too."

"That part does sorta suck."

Matt parked and they went in, intending to go up to the room to shower and get ready for services. A small cluster of people at the reception desk moved to the side and Lee spotted Tony. "I'll be right up," he said, touching Matt's sleeve and pointing.

"I'll wait." Matt veered toward one of the chairs in the lobby and Lee pressed on, going right to his Senior's side.

"You look good," he said softly. "A little older, a lot hotter."

The desk clerk gave him a look, but Tony just gathered him in close and kissed his temple. "Are you okay?"

"Why does everyone keep asking me that? I'm as well as the rest of you."

"That rough?" Tony leaned back to study him. Tony was still beautiful, Lee thought as he studied right back. There were creases at the corner of his eyes, but other than that he could still have been a twenty-one year old college senior. "You look tired."

"Matt's here." Lee rolled his eyes. "And I'm pretty sure that if I hadn't been in need of best friend stuff he would have picked up a brother for his very own. Even temporarily."

"That's our Matt." Tony laughed, both of them knowing that Matt talked a good game but had the same level of respect for his family in him that they all did. Tony looked over and waved to Matt. "He looks like he had best friend duty until dawn."

"I'm fine."

"Where's Joey?"

"Not here. Long story. Well, short story." Lee rolled his eyes. "He has issues with death, apparently. It's nice to know he's completely human; here I thought I was falling in love with a perfect man."

The world slid slightly to the right and Tony dragged him across the lobby to Matt. "You. Watch him. I have to finish checking in. Do we have time for a glass of wine before we all need to change?"

"Uh, if we're fast." Matt was eyeing them both warily. "Hi, Tony."

"Hey, Matt." Tony leaned down and kissed Matt's cheek. "Pour something white into him. I'll be right there."

Lee shook his head. "No. Both of you just stop. Right now." He took Tony's hand and squeezed it. "This is about Ken. Not me. Okay?"

Tony looked torn, but Matt was nodding.

"Tony. We'll talk later. After the memorial, after we've pulled as many men wearing our pins as we can, after we've done right by our brother. Then we'll talk about the state of my heart. Right now, there's more important things." Lee nodded firmly and aimed Tony at the front desk. "Check in. We'll see you at the chapel."

With all apparent reluctance, Tony relented. "Okay, Lee. Your call."

"My call." Lee looked at Matt. "You want to shower first or me?"

"You can." Matt stood up and pulled his key card out of his pocket. "You need a ride to campus, Tony?"

"Nah, I got it. See you both in a little bit. Hey, Lee?"

"Yeah."

"You can still fall in love with him. Even if he's got issues."

Lee rolled his eyes. "I know. Drop it for now, okay?"

"Ohh." Matt's eyes went wide, but as soon as Lee turned to glare at him he mimed zipping his mouth closed and smiling innocently.

"Come on." Lee rolled his eyes so hard they hurt and headed to the elevator. "Jeeze. A man can't have some personal growth without hearing about it from y'all."

Matt tittered but left him alone about it all the way up to the room and for the entire time they spent getting ready.

"Do you know how long the service is going to be?" Lee asked. He was checking himself in the full length mirror while Matt tied his necktie. Lee's dinner jacket looked okay; his tie was in the CSUC colors and his pants held a crease. He couldn't really ask for more, he thought. Not sharp, but definitely better than he'd been able to pull off for his own graduation.

"Don't know—how long do memorials usually go? About forty-five minutes?" Matt finished with his tie and pulled on his suit jacket, then picked up his ball cap.

"You're not—"

"Dude. No." Matt rolled his eyes and carefully took his lapel pin off the hat and put it where it belonged. "Let me look at you."

Lee let him look and even let Matt straighten his already perfectly straight lapel pin. "Can we go now?"

"Yes." Matt gave Lee's cheek a pat. "Call Joey first. Once more. Try his cell."

Lee looked at him for a long moment and then shook his head. "Only for you or Tony would I do this."

"And René."

"And René." Lee took out his phone and called Joey's cell. "Out of range or off," he reported a moment later. Then he deliberately turned off his phone and tossed it on the bed. "Let's go."

Matt nodded. "I'm sorry, bro."

Lee took Matt's hand and tangled their fingers together. "Can we just... not? For now." He didn't want to worry about why Joey wasn't picking up, not then.

"Yeah." Matt kept holding his hand, all the way down to the car.

Lee looked out the window as they drove. The town looked like any other college town: students, sunshine and green leaves. It didn't seem right to Lee that there wasn't an outward sign that the world was suddenly poorer by one good soul. There should have been a mark, somewhere, an open wound.

Matt held his hand again.

Together they walked to the chapel and joined the other people gathering, looking around for pins on lapels or faces they knew. Denied the chance to really linger, and not wanting to draw attention to themselves, they went in and took their places in the rapidly filling space.

"It's a nice chapel," Lee said, looking around.

"Of course it is. He helped to design it." Matt smiled sadly, and they sat back to read the order of service and prepare themselves.

Matt's estimate of forty-five minutes was about right, and Lee found himself grateful that it didn't go on for much more than that. He was by turns grateful that the prayers and hymns were chosen to reflect peace and sunshine and life after death, and utterly horrified that the words spoken could have been about any of them. There wasn't anything about the service that meant Ken to him, aside from the mentions of his legacy, found in stone and glass and steel all around them, and around the country.

There was talk of his family, his parents and brothers. No words of comfort for a loving partner. No solace for his chosen, secret brotherhood.

190

Matt's hand in his, a hand from behind placed on Lee's shoulder; that was the real comfort. Lee looked back and smiled at Carrigan, grateful for the warmth in the man's eyes.

Finally, the last hymn had been sung and the pastor had said his final words of comfort, then walked from the chapel, out into the sunlight with Ken's family behind him. The congregation followed, people talking quietly, a few people sobbing.

"Do you see Tony?" Matt asked, craning his neck.

"No. But I see Echo." Lee edged forward, angling them across the flow of people exiting the chapel. He missed, but not before Echo had seen him and indicated that he'd wait outside, and not before Matt had seen someone else wearing a tiny triangular pin.

"I have no idea how we're going to manage to find everyone," Matt whispered as they got outside and headed for a tree not far away, but out of the path of people trying to leave. A few other people seemed to have the same idea, and small clusters of people began to form. "Have you seen Kirk yet?"

Lee looked around, adding Kirk to his list. "Not yet. Did you text him earlier?"

"Yeah, but I was hoping to actually see him, you know? Give him a hug, touch base." Matt sighed and they kept an eye out, watching people move around in those little groups.

The vast majority were obviously colleagues or family, making plans and talking in hushed tones, and they shifted, taking in more individuals as others moved away. But Lee watched as a lone man took a careful look around and approached another, his hand out. The same scene played out twice more, and Lee was about to ask Matt if he'd seen Tony or Echo, both of whom were lost in the clusters, when a very young man walked up to them.

"My name is Ezra," he said calmly, hand out. His pin was firmly in place and his hair had been so recently trimmed that he had a white space at his hairline. "You're invited to come to the house. Your brothers would like to comfort you, and supper will be served for everyone following a short meeting."

"Lee Sutton. Thank you," Lee said, automatically shaking his hand. "We'll be there."

Ezra nodded and shook Matt's hand as well. "All sixteen of us are here, trying to catch everyone. Please pass the word."

"Of course." Matt looked faintly stunned, but very impressed. "Can we bring anything?"

Shaking his head, Ezra told them to come by whenever they were ready, that street parking would be allowed. Then he left, presumably to find more brothers.

"Well." Lee looked at Matt. "I wonder how they cleared the parking thing?"

"I'm telling you. The founders have some kind of pull, man."

Tony walked toward them, followed by another three men, none of whom looked familiar to Lee. He paid attention to the introductions and promptly forgot their names.

"Lee?" Tony wore his concern like another layer of clothing.

"I'm sorry," Lee apologized. "I'm really not dealing with all this very well." He sighed and leaned into Tony's body, accepting the half-hug. "If Matt's willing, I'd like to just go over to the house. Oh, I saw Echo. And Carrigan, someone needs to find him and make sure he knows."

"He's found and he's riding with Dominic." One of the new faces gave Lee a sympathetic pat. "We'll see you all there. Tony?"

"I'll ride with my Junior." Tony's arm tightened around

Lee's shoulders.

Two voices plus Lee's murmured, "Possessive." Lee added, "Peter's gonna have my balls, man, you keep this up."

Tony just snorted and steered Lee after Matt. "What're you driving these days, Matt? I'm not riding in a Civic."

"Bite me," Matt said mildly, pointing out his newish Impala. "Be glad I didn't bring my half restored Mustang. Or the old Jeep. Get in and cuddle Lee up."

Lee rolled his eyes. "I don't cuddle."

A body detached itself from the shade of a tree and walked toward them. "He's lying. He cuddles all the time. Hello, Tony."

Lee stopped walking. "Joey." He wasn't surprised by the relief he felt, though he wasn't precisely delighted to have his suspicions about his feelings confirmed in such a manner. He drank in the sight of Joey in a dark suit, unconsciously and unwillingly adding up the cost of it by the tailoring and fabric and deciding that he liked the narrow cut of the shoulder on Joey but not on anyone else. "You came."

Tony's arm was still around his shoulder. "Obviously," he said without any hurtfulness in his voice. "Are you going to hug him first or am I? I could really call seniority, but I'll let you take first blood if you want."

A laugh startled out of Lee, sharp and brittle, and all three of them took a step closer to him, even Tony, who was already well within Lee's personal space. "I'm fine," Lee said automatically.

Joey nodded and came closer, close enough that Tony backed away a few steps. "I left early this morning," he said, one hand coming up to cup Lee's jaw. "I'm sorry. I really am."

"We'll talk later." Lee spoke softly. "I'm not mad at you. I'm glad you're here, though."

"Me, too." Joey kissed his mouth softly. "I talked to Echo yesterday. He told me about how Ken helped you when your grandmother passed away. I didn't know."

Lee took Joey's hand, peripherally aware that Matt and Tony had backed off and were leaning on the hood of Matt's car, watching them. "It's not about that," Lee said slowly. "Ken really did help me, it's true. He held my hand, he stayed with me, he ran interference when I had to plan the funeral and get Gram's house on the market. He even helped me with the mechanics of how to pay off all her debts with the insurance and made sure there wasn't anything outstanding." Lee nodded, a lot more sure of what he was trying to say, exactly. "But I'm not here because of that, and I don't feel this strongly because he helped me. I was—am—closer to Matt and Tony and even René than I was to Ken. But he was a brother and he chose to leave us. We failed him, somehow. I would feel like this if it were any of the brothers I shared time with."

"Okay." Joey's gaze roamed over Lee's face. "I hear what you're saying. I admire it and I love that you're so tied to those feelings. I have deep feelings, too, but I handle them differently."

"I get that." Lee kissed Joey softly. "I do. It's only been a few weeks, Joey. You and me, we're building something together and it's good. We just don't know each other well enough yet to navigate this sort of thing smoothly, is all. It's just too soon. That doesn't mean we won't get there. I think we will. That you're here, now, tells me that."

"I knew Ken." Joey's eyes grew distant as he looked into the middle distance. "I liked him very much. I'm here for him." He focused on Lee's face. "But I'm here because of you. Does that make sense?"

"Yeah." Lee squeezed Joey's hand and nodded. "Yeah,

it does. Thank you."

Tony cleared his throat and smiled pointedly at them. "Okay? Can I just...? For a moment."

Lee rolled his eyes. "Yes. But I get him back later."

"More than that, the four of us—five, if Matt wants to play—are going to sit down and have a long chat. You and me, Joey and Echo, Matt." Tony nodded firmly, then pushed himself off of Matt's bumper to fold Joey into a tight hug. "You look smokin' in this suit."

Joey laughed, hugging him back. "It's my interview suit."

"I'd hire you." Tony kissed Joey's cheek loudly before he let him step back. "You look great, seriously."

Joey smiled. "You, too. How's Peter?"

Lee and Matt exchanged glances and rolled their eyes. "Did you hear that? A family meeting. How old am I?"

"Fourteen," Matt told him matter of factly. "Deal with it."

"I wonder if they're going to discuss 'intentions'?" Lee asked him, ignoring the way that Joey and Tony were watching him and Matt talking about them.

Matt shrugged one shoulder. "Joey's dad—I mean Senior, sorry—isn't here. But he's got Echo, so I expect that all the questions about picking life partners will be covered."

"Echo likes me."

"Echo likes everyone."

Tony cleared his throat. "All right. Sorry. Jeeze. Just trying to help."

Lee took pity on him, too tired and too wrung out to play games. "Joey, we're going to the house. TCF are opening the doors."

"Yeah, I talked to some pretty little thing named Ezra. Were we ever that young?"

"You weren't," Tony said with a grin. "Lee wasn't.

Matt was."

"Hey." Matt held up his car keys. "I'm driving. Pile in, y'all."

Lee looked at Joey, waiting.

"Ride with me?" Joey inclined his head down the row of cars. "I know the way."

Lee smiled faintly. "Yeah. I think I know where it is, too, if you get lost." He took Joey's hand and glanced at Matt and Tony. "See you there. We'll be right behind you."

They weren't, though, since by the time they'd gotten into Joey's car and joined the queue of cars leaving the parking lot, Matt and Tony were long gone.

"Did you get here in time to get a room at a hotel?" Lee asked, once more watching the town out of the car window.

"No. I barely made it to the service." Joey drove, his gaze on the road. "It was packed. Standing room at the back."

Lee nodded. "Good. That's good." Ken deserved more than that, though. He deserved to have found help. "I'm glad you're here."

"I'm glad I'm with you." Joey had to let go of his hand in order to make a turn, but otherwise he held Lee's hand all the way to the house.

As they'd been told, there didn't seem to be an issue with them parking along the street. The residential area wasn't exactly a high traffic zone, but Lee had never seen it lined with cars before. He assumed that the mansions all had ample parking in their drives. They stopped in front of a mansion across the street and down the road a short way, then walked back to the narrow drive leading to the house of The Chosen Family, passing Matt's car on the way. Unsurprisingly, the small parking area there was full.

Walking into the house was surreal, in keeping with the feel of the entire trip. Instead of a wide and empty entryway lined with neat hooks holding robes, coats and book bags, there was a group of people milling about, some joking about how they all wanted to use their old hooks, and others simply going to what used to be their space and looking baffled, as if time had slipped away without them noticing.

Lee was as human as the rest of them, and while he didn't actually go to his hook, he did look that way, unsurprised to find it occupied by someone's suit jacket. "Hey," he said, his hand on Joey's elbow. "I'll be in there. You're about to be mobbed by old friends."

"I'm what?" Joey gave him a fast, confused look, but within seconds he was pulled into a tight hug by the man Lee had seen bearing down on them. "Aaron!"

"Joey. God, it's good to see you. Come on, Craig and Diego are getting into the bean dip."

"Sure." Joey looked poleaxed. "Oh, hey, wait. Lee, this is Aaron. He was a year ahead of me. Aaron, this is my boyfriend, Lee Sutton. Lee is Tony Sanchez' Junior."

"No shit?"

Lee shook hands and touched Joey again. "Find me later, okay? Say hi to everyone, I'll be around."

"Okay." Joey kept him there long enough to kiss once more. "Don't leave without me."

Lee smiled and left him there with the throng in the entry. Tony and Matt were likely deeper into the house by then. He headed toward the pool table almost out of habit.

There were about thirty-five men there, Lee estimated, and he suspected that the sixteen active members of TCF were not mingling. In fact, the ages of those Lee could see as he made his way through the room ranged from around twenty-five to sixty. True, there wasn't a huge percentage of men over forty, but they were there, talking quietly to brothers who were much younger than themselves.

Connecting.

All the furniture had been rearranged, which wasn't particularly surprising; the tables were against the walls and he could see snack foods laid out, though nothing that looked like the meal that Ezra had mentioned. That would probably come after the meeting. Also, the couches and chairs were well away from the circle design on the floor. Another, closer look showed that the lines that marked the quarters of the circle had been extended outward with masking tape, so that each quarter held not only the ritual space but a very large area behind that, containing the seating.

Lee was pondering that and its implications when he heard his name.

"Lee Sutton." An older man was smiling at him, his face tantalizingly familiar. "I had no idea."

Lee stared hard and then his eyes went wide. "Dr. Lowry!" He held out his hand. "Wow." The thought of any of his own professors being members had never once crossed his mind. "What year did you graduate?"

"1973." Dr. Lowry shook his hand, then winked and pointed to his left. "Dr. Noonan is over there. He was class of '67."

"Dude." Lee blinked. "Wow."

"It's a college town." Dr. Lowry shrugged. "We go to school, we get degrees, we get jobs. For some of us that doesn't mean we leave home, is all."

Lee nodded. "When you put it that way, I'm surprised there aren't more profs here, then."

"TCF is selective." Dr. Lowry smiled at him. "What are you up to these days? Still interested in politics?"

"I'm at Legacy, writing my dissertation." Lee began to fill him in, pausing when Tony walked past and gave his arm a squeeze on his way to the bowl of corn chips. "After that, I'm not sure where I'll be," Lee said. "There are two research positions I'm eyeing, but it might be better for me to go overseas instead for a couple of years."

"There should be a way to research there and be working for a university or college here, I would think. God knows that the political landscape is shifting more and more rapidly and having ripple effects that reach further than ever—"

"Gentlemen. If I may have your attention?"

Dr. Lowry broke off as a deep and carrying voice seemed to fill the room. Lee smiled and turned to face the center of the circle, knowing who would be there.

"Thank you." Echo smiled around himself as everyone fell silent. "My name is Echo, and I graduated with the class of 2000. Someone told the current Speaker that I have a big mouth, I think. I'd blame my Senior, but he's been busy catching up with old friends."

There was polite laughter and Lee looked around for Joey, finally spotting him near the entryway. He hadn't gotten very far.

"I've been asked to explain briefly what's about to happen." Echo pointed to the floor. "As you can see, the quarters have been extended and seating has been arranged in each section. The Brotherhood of Leuce asks that you go to your quarters and sit with those of your line. This is to symbolize our duty—both to our assigned roles and to each other as brothers. We all had our family lines; we still do. But we are all one Family, and we share in something great. When we're all seated—some of us lucky enough to have our erastes or eromenos or even both with us—the active members will join us. They ask that we make ourselves as comfortable as we wish. After all, we're home."

There was a low murmur of voices as men moved,

talking quietly, calling to brothers as they found places to sit. Lee told Dr. Lowry that they'd speak again later, and went to find Tony. If he couldn't hold Joey's hand, he'd press Tony into the promised cuddle.

In a few moments things settled down, and Lee leaned against Tony's arm. He looked around, smiling when he saw that Matt had his arms looped around Kirk whom he'd obviously located at some point, possibly near the pool table. Lee had no idea what to expect, particularly, but he felt more comforted there, in the house with Tony and Matt and Joey and Echo, than he had at the chapel.

If Lee had a religion, it seemed to be based upon security and unconditional love. He wondered why so many times he'd missed finding that inside a church.

In the deepening silence, he heard the door to the outside open and measured steps of many feet. As one, the men seated in the circle turned to watch sixteen young men come to them in groups of four.

They had their robes on, but their heads were uncovered, the cowled hoods loose around their shoulders, and they didn't wear their masks. The oldest students came first, the four of them parting and going to stand in their quarters as the next set came to join them, until all sixteen were standing in the center of the room, facing inward, their heads bowed.

Ezra was with Pins, Lee noted absently.

One of the Speakers stepped forward. "Sit, brothers," he said quietly, and the fifteen robed figures sank to the floor. "Brothers. All of our brothers. The Chosen Family welcomes you all home."

Most nodded, some murmured low words of thanks. Lee was mesmerized.

"I'm Brian." He looked around, his face serious and his hands by his side. He looked like he could have been an athlete, but he held himself like a young man used to public speaking. "We gather in sadness today. We gather here to say good bye and find peace and comfort with those we trust. And we gather with questions."

He began to move, walking very slowly, so that he could see everyone in the circle as he spoke. "The first question I had when we met two days ago at the suggestion of my Junior, who wanted to do something for all of us, was to see if the house had ever opened like this before. And then we questioned if it mattered if anyone had done it before—we wanted to. We are here now and we knew that there would be brothers coming. We wanted to let you know that your ties are still active, that those who took the vows before you and after you are all your brothers. That in your grief, we would be here for you. Always.

"The Chosen Family has lost brothers before. To war. To AIDS. To car accidents. To domestic violence. To heart disease and cancer." He took another step and looked around the still room. "There is no ritual within the Brotherhood for passing. We do not think, at this time, that we'd like to change that. But we did very much want to have a meeting with as many of you as possible.

"We have a fifty year history. We have had sadness and broken hearts. But we now have anger as well, and remorse and questions."

Brian's shoulders went back a little more. "I wasn't lucky enough to meet Ken Hayes. But he was a brother and he could have walked in that door and talked to any of us. He chose not to. None of us—none of us—can possibly know what he was going through, what he was thinking or feeling, and I would never claim that I could have solved his problems or helped in any way other than to listen. That may very well not have been enough. Sometimes having a listening ear doesn't make anything better nor lend strength.

"But it might have. This time, it might have."

Lee nodded, his eyes burning. He would have listened. He would have gone to Ken and held him and talked to him.

"As far as we know," Brian said quietly, "Ken did not call upon any brother. That might be simply a lack of information on my part, but no one has said otherwise, no one has passed the word. If I'm wrong, I apologize, sincerely."

No one said anything. No one moved. Beside Lee, Tony was still and warm.

"My brothers here in front of you, the active members... we're angry. We are mad at Ken for not reaching out. We're mad that it's not easier for any of us to reach out, that's it actually difficult to find you all. We couldn't find any of you until we were at the memorial service or by phoning our Seniors and hoping they were in contact with their friends. So we have a proposal for you."

He turned and looked around as if searching for someone. "Ez."

Ezra stood up, his face pink. "I'm Ezra." He cleared his throat and Lee smiled slightly at the resulting squeak. "Fifty years ago the record book was in its infancy. It's a wonderful thing, and it serves its purpose beautifully. We are not proposing that it be changed in any way. We would, however, like to create a virtual appendix of sorts."

When Ezra glanced at Brian, Lee could see how nervous the young man was, and felt sorry for him. It couldn't be easy, looking at a room full of men and suggesting they change long standing traditions.

"Go ahead," Brian said softly. "We agree with you."

Ezra nodded once and took a deep breath. "We would like to create a list of all the brothers, the names taken from the record book, and what contact information we can find or have provided to us. This list will be encrypted on a dedicated server that has been made available to us. That means that while the information will be online, it will not be accessible to anyone but us, ever. You will not get spam e-mail, you will not be compromised, you will not be outed. That is of primary importance—I'm not out of the closet, I would never be part of something that could accidentally cause someone's life to change."

Lee glanced at Tony and found him looking thoughtful, which was mirrored on many other faces. Some were already nodding.

"This online space will be password protected. The contact information—addresses, phone numbers, e-mails, whatever we're provided with or can verify on our own through search engines—will not be posted. Even when you log onto the site, you won't be able to look up your friends and see their e-mail addresses. You may contact the webmaster and give your information to be passed along. All you will see when you log on will be a list of names—those for which we have contact details. The only person who will ever contact you on behalf of the Brotherhood will be the current webmaster or a brother you've given us permission to forward your number to. If you give blanket permission, we'll pass your number to any brother who asks." Ezra was speaking more confidently, his excitement for the project growing more evident. "In the future, if there is a clear wish expressed, we might be able to set up message boards and that sort of thing; right now we're just making the space as secure as possible. The list and the site will become the duty of the Record Keeper, getting help as needed from the other brothers; some people are better with computers than others."

That brought more than a few chuckles, especially from the older brothers.

Brian smiled and nodded, one of his hands on Ezra's shoulders. "So, that's what we'd like to do. For you, for us, for the guys coming up behind us. I'd like to open the floor to questions and comments. Anyone?"

"I have a comment." The voice came from the doorway to the entry and the surprise on Brian's face made Lee turn to look, more than the voice or statement did. A man stood there, wearing a robe that was black and heavy, almost the same as the others but not quite. It was longer, tied at the waist with a long blue sash instead of the plain woven ties Lee's friends had all used, and his hood was up, covering his head and face. In one hand was a small book, on his robe was a tiny gold triangle, and in his other hand he held up a house key.

There was a very low murmur that spread through the room like a wave, and then Dr. Lowry stood up. Seconds later so did the man beside him, then another, and then Lee and Tony and Echo until everyone was standing, staring.

Brian, to his credit, did them all proud. "Brother. You are welcome in our house. And we are honored."

"I'm the one who is honored. Please, gentlemen. Sit. Don't embarrass an old man." He waved a hand and slowly they all sat down again, except for Brian. The hooded figure walked to him and reached out, putting one hand on Brian's shoulder. "Brother," he said with a thick voice. "It's been too long since I said that."

Brian, his eyes shining, slowly returned the gesture. "But you are," he said with a smile. "Our brother."

The man lifted his hand and pushed back his hood to reveal a shock of unruly white hair and a kind, lined face. He looked around at all of them, the shine of his eyes not dimming no matter how rapidly he blinked. "My name," he said as he looked around at all of them, "Is Milo Stephen Hunt. I graduated in the year nineteen fifty-nine, and I was one of the first four members of the Brotherhood of Leuce. You are my legacy. Each of you. I could not possibly be more proud."

Lee lifted a hand to his face, not at all surprised to find that the pounding of his heart had resulted in watery eyes. He wasn't alone.

"My comments are threefold." Milo Hunt turned slowly, looking at them all. "I think that these young men have the very best intentions for the Brotherhood. Times change and we must change as well, lest all will be lost. I sincerely hope that you will encourage them in this endeavor. I will give them my phone number. Second—if any of you need a brother, I expect you to use it. The choice that Ken Hayes made should only be considered when you are utterly bereft. As long as there is breath in my body, none of you are alone." Again, there were nods of agreement, and Milo nodded firmly, though his voice had wavered with emotion as he spoke. He cleared his throat and carried on. "And finally, it has become plain to me the last few years that I must do my part to protect The Chosen Family to the best of my ability; merely making this space available isn't enough when time is leaning upon me. One day I will no longer live in the big monstrosity of a house that hides this one from the street. We must make provisions. By which I mean, any lawyers present may find me over by the salsa when the meeting is adjourned. This house will always be here for you all. I promise you."

Lee wasn't sure who started the applause. It might have spontaneously erupted, as everyone was clapping and there were even a few cheers. In a moment or two Brian held up both of his hands, calling for silence, but they kept applauding until he whistled sharply.

"Thank you," he said, beaming at the first of the brothers. "Sincerely and completely." Applause immediately threatened to break out again, but Brian lifted his hand once more. "May I take it that the active members have the support of those present to go forward with our project?"

That time he let the applause carry them for a few moments. "Thank you. We have a sheet ready for you all to sign up with the information you want to share and any limits you'd like on the dissemination of your numbers. We'll be in touch with each of you in coming weeks as we work on this. For now, I'd like to once more offer my condolences to you all. I'm deeply sorry for your loss."

He stepped back to the center of the circle, only a pace or two, and gestured for Milo Hunt to join him. "Thank you all for coming. Meeting adjourned." The robed brothers stood up, and all around the room men started talking and moving, pushing chairs back and standing up.

Lee looked at Tony and leaned in again, slipping under his arm. "Hey. That was pretty amazing. Milo, man," he whispered. Then he looked hard at Tony and asked, "How are you?" He hadn't asked until then, swamped in his own feelings.

"Well." Tony looked around and sighed. The others were mingling, many going to talk to Ezra and Brian, some moving to Milo with awed faces. "I miss him. I'm angry, like Brian said. And I'm very, very blessed to have you here."

Lee nodded. "Yeah. All of that." He put his own arms around Tony, hugging him and listening to his heart beat. "All of that."

Chapter Sixteen
Family Meeting, Redux

They were still cuddled up when Echo and Joey came to find them. Lee had felt a few tremors that could have been Tony wanting to grieve, but when he looked at Tony's face he was dry-eyed. Still, Lee didn't want to leave him simply to find his boyfriend; he and Joey would have a lot of time to talk on the way home.

"We need to talk."

Lee sighed and would have objected except it was Echo and not Joey looking at him with stern eyes. So stern, in fact, that Lee didn't move. He liked having his Senior's arm around him; it felt safe, and judging by Echo's expression it would be wise to stay safe. "I only mussed him a little, and the whole naked swimming thing was his idea. And he brought the booze."

Joey's cheeks flushed and Lee laughed softly. "Note to self. Joey blushes when his Junior hears about his sex life."

"Hush, you." Joey reached out a hand for Lee's. "And Echo wants to talk to us about sleeping arrangements, not what you and I do when left to our own devices."

Tony let Lee go and gave Echo a grin. "Do we all get

to play this game? I'll warn you, Peter is open-minded."

"I'm in theater, honey." Echo winked. "I would melt your Peter's mind."

Lee didn't doubt it for a minute. "I need to find Matt. Since we're sharing a room he should be in on Echo's orgy plan."

Three people turned around to look at them and Echo made a strangled noise. "Harper Lee Sutton—"

"Only Matt and Tony are allowed to call me that."

"Harper Lee?" Joey looked delighted.

Tony sighed. "This conversation is off the rails, and I hereby declare that we'll discuss rooms and how to get Lee and Joey into a shared one, later." He stood up and walked away, toward the corn chips.

Echo watched him go and shrugged. "All right, then. See you guys at the hotel bar later tonight. I'm going to go talk to Milo. How cool is that?"

Lee moved over on the big chair to make a space for Joey, then looked around instead. "There's a couch free, if you want to sit."

Joey nodded, but before they could move to it Matt bounded up, dragging a man with him. "Lee! Look!"

"Cesar!" Lee reached for him and within moments he and Joey had agreed that talking could wait until they were back at the hotel. There were too many long-lost friends to lose the chance at catching up.

"The setting isn't ideal anyway," Joey said with a laugh. He leaned in and kissed Lee's mouth. "I'm going to go find Craig again, and that information sheet Brian and Ezra were talking about."

Lee nodded. "Put my phone number on there, too—and my cell."

Cesar was looking at them both, from Lee to Joey and back, and when Joey left he pinned Lee with a sharp look. "He's a honey. Spill."

Laughing, Lee started to spill, Matt filling in the blanks as he talked.

For an hour or so, Lee talked with whoever wandered into his range. He saw Carrigan and they had an involved discussion about how to properly construct a seven layer dip, and then Tony came by with his version. Someone started writing it all down.

Supper was catered, hot dishes and extra plates being carried in by a staff of ten or so; the conversations in the room all shifting slightly to account for ears that were not initiated. Lee thought that perhaps everyone was relieved that the staff wasn't staying to serve; once all the food was laid out and the plates stacked, they left again.

The party—for now it was a proper wake, even though there wasn't any alcohol—kept going until after dark, when people started making their way to the coat hooks. Joey and Lee collected Echo, who had flown in but not rented a car, and found Matt and Tony so they could all thank the host brothers.

"It wasn't a good reason for a reunion," Brian said, shaking their hands. "But I'm glad that we could help in some way."

"Y'all are going to help in huge ways," Matt told him. "You're doing a great job."

Brian glanced around and smiled when he saw Ezra. "It was him, mostly. He feels things in a very big way, and then he does stuff about it."

Tony and Lee exchanged looks, and Joey said, "He's your Junior, huh?"

"Yeah." Brian looked faintly embarrassed. "He's a good kid."

"Keep in touch with him," Matt advised. Then he winked. "Don't let him get away." Then he walked away, leaving Brian to stammer out a good bye to the next person leaving.

"That was mean," Echo said, grinning.

"Boy's got it bad." Matt grinned right back. "I was helping."

"You help a lot." Echo gave Matt a significant look and tilted his head toward Lee and Joey. "Going to help them?"

"They don't need my help," Matt said airily. "Because they're going to sit down with us in a booth at the hotel bar, and we're going to trade stories until they both understand what's what."

"Oh, Lord." Lee rolled his eyes and pulled on Joey's hand. "That's our cue. Ready?"

"More than ready. See you, guys." He waved with his other hand and the two of them left, walking toward the street.

"In the bar," Tony called out. "Right?"

"Yes, Dad." Lee shook his head. "Honestly. Like they wouldn't be able to find us."

"Right, me without a room and you sharing with Matt. They'd find us."

"And be horrible to us."

"Mmmhmm." Joey looked at him as they walked, and smiled a little ruefully. "They're convinced that we need to talk, you know."

Lee sighed. "Yeah. And I suppose we do, a little. But not like they're going to make it." They turned off the driveway and onto the sidewalk. "Tony, especially. He'll tell stories, lay all of me out there for you to see. And then he'll tell you what it all means, where it all comes from. He'll give you my behaviors, what causes them, what the best way to handle them is. And he'll do it because he cares and he wants me—us—to be happy."

"Sure, of course." Joey nodded. "But the thing is— that's what a relationship is. We've known each other for what, less than a month? We're supposed to discover things for ourselves, nice and gradual." He laughed softly. "How do you feel about a preemptive strike?"

Lee considered. "Define."

"You and me in my car, away from people. We can talk about what needs discussing—if anything. Without our family in the middle of it, guiding us along like it's an intervention."

Lee squeezed Joey's hand and they crossed the street to the car. "I like the way you think, Dr. Reed."

"And then we can go parking."

Lee laughed. "We'll see."

They drove back to the campus without talking about it, and Joey parked the car in the back lot behind the student union building. There were trees there, and while the buildings were close, it felt like they were isolated.

"It's a good thing you're not one for tiny sports cars," Lee said. He pushed the passenger seat way back and tilted the backrest so he could recline comfortably.

"I can't afford one of those," Joey said, rolling his eyes while he adjusted his seat, too. "Sensible is more my range."

"Non-existent is mine." Lee twisted his mouth. "And there's my particular issue again."

"Which?"

Lee let out a breath. "Here's the thing. The one flashing big warning about being involved with me."

"That sounds ominous." Joey smiled at him and settled back. "Hit me with it."

Lee scratched a non-existent itch on his head, one that matched his current car budget, and said, "I can pretty much promise you that money will never not be an issue with me. It's something I can try really, really hard to keep to myself, but I will always, always notice things and measure by money." That sounded horrible, even to him, and he tried again. "I see things, and meet people, and everything is just automatically noted. Who has it, who wants it, how they earn it, how it's spent. I'm one of those guys who's working his ass off to be dining in restaurants where you drop five hundred dollars on a meal without blinking, but inside I'll be screaming about how much money it's costing and how long I could have eaten on that by buying groceries."

He turned his head to look out the window, feeling oddly sick as he talked. It wasn't like he didn't know all of it; it was about himself and he'd had a lot of time to figure it out. He'd taken the psych classes, he'd been friends with Matt, who honestly couldn't tell one brand of anything from another, unless it was cars. And Matt didn't care. Status and social standings and appearing to be successful never mattered to him.

"I grew up poor and wanting, determined to move myself into a social class that has what I didn't," Lee said softly. "It's... I'm a snob. And I resent other snobs. This has created some interesting social issues. I don't do well with people, anyway—Matt says I only have half the social skills of other people—and I tend to quietly resent everyone for either being low class or for being high class. I'm probably the most judgmental person you will ever meet and the quickest way to hurt me to the bone is to imply that I don't know something, understand something, or value something because I'm poor. Too often poor is equated with stupid. I won't appear stupid for any longer than I can help it."

From the other side of the car was a resounding silence.

"So, there you go." Lee swallowed hard, his face getting hot and his stomach trying to roll over. A damp patch was forming at the small of his back. "I'm materialistic and judgmental, and I could probably go through your closet and show you how many shirts you have that cost more than a hundred and seventy dollars."

"Lee." Joey's voice was soft, too. "So what if you notice that stuff? So what if you want things and to be recognized as someone who earns enough to afford them? I think that it's in a lot of people's nature to want to acquire objects, and it's definitely a human condition to want both approval and to be acknowledged." Joey's hand touched Lee's, just stroked his fingers. "You're a hell of a lot more than simply that set of feelings, you know."

"Yeah, I know." Lee glanced over at him and rolled his eyes. "Of course I am. But this is a part of me, too, and I don't think it's going to go away. But I can keep it to myself when we go out and I'm mentally totaling up how much your friends' art collection is worth and not make you endure my envy."

"I get envy. All the time." Joey lifted his hand to Lee's jaw and turned his face so they were looking at each other. "You're the one who dropped absolutely everything to be here. You're fiercely loyal to people, even those you've never met. You are the epitome of what we're supposed to be. You have an open heart, and you throw yourself into life without holding back. I should know. Look what we've done. Look how much we feel, the two of us, in a short time." He smiled.

Lee smiled, too, and kissed Joey's mouth gently, lingering a little. "I'm here, too. Giving you the first warning talk I've ever given anyone. Usually I let guys figure it out on their own."

"How's that worked out for you?" Joey kissed him back, his lips soft.

"Not as well as this." Lee took a breath, sighed and sat back. "Mind you, I've never had Tony hovering like this. He's relentless." Lee considered for a moment and then said, "I told Tony I thought I was falling in love with a perfect man."

Joey snorted. "And now that I took two days to make myself come and be a supportive boyfriend, if I couldn't bring myself to be a proper brother?"

Lee looked at him. "Now I think I'm falling in love with a normal human. Well, a really, really hot and smart normal human. You came through, Joey. I know I should feel bad about being happy you forced yourself to come, but I'm just glad you're here."

Joey sighed. "I'm completely aware that how I handle death and funerals isn't normal. I mean, I know it in my heart, not just my head. I bet everyone's been asking you where the hell I was."

Lee could hardly deny that.

"And," Joey went on, "I know that you've been confused and probably hurt by it."

"No," Lee protested. "No, no."

"Yes." Joey gave him a stern look. "I know it's odd. I know that it's peculiar. And now I know another thing. I know that it's far more important to me that I be here, supporting you when you need me, than it is that I be at home saying good bye alone. Who knows? Maybe mourning is actually easier if there's someone to hold your hand through it."

Lee smiled and kissed Joey's cheek. "I appreciate that it was hard for you to come here. I'm absolutely delighted that you did it for me." He kissed Joey's cheek again, closer to his mouth, and then again, laying a trail.

"If you keep doing that you're going to get laid." Lee sounded amused and a little hopeful.

Lee turned his head and kissed Joey's mouth, far less tenderly than he had been doing up to that point. There was a certain note of desperation in the kiss he got back, and both he and Joey were struggling to move; car seats and suit jackets weren't making things easier on either of them.

"We should've taken Matt's car," Lee said, stroking Joey's hair and making himself not bury his hand in it. That would lead to pulling hair and harder kisses and then they'd be stuck with nowhere to take things, since Joey's car wasn't built for making out like teenagers.

"We should probably go to the Dunkirk." Joey wasn't backing off, though. In fact, his hands were busy petting and burrowing under Lee's dinner jacket, then tugging at buttons.

"They're going to be phoning us really soon," Lee said, nodding. He leaned back and started trying to get his jacket off, sucking in his stomach to let Joey pull Lee's shirt free from his trousers. "Matt'll be pissed when he remembers I left my phone in the room."

"Mine's dead and I forgot the car charger." Joey half-turned and did something to the steering column, making the wheel lift up a crucial two inches. "You watch out the window."

"If we get arrested Tony will fucking kill me." Lee pulled his shirt up and out of the way, working on his belt while Joey did the button and zipper.

"Only after he finishes with me. Keep a look out." Warm hands pushed at fabric and petted Lee's cock through his boxers. "And you might want to not yell."

Lee snorted out a laugh and then gasped as Joey freed his cock from layers of clothes. "I'll try. Can't promise." He watched as Joey's fingers slid over him, far too lightly, and remembered he was supposed to be looking out the window. "Joey."

"Shh." Joey bent and went down on him, sucking hard.

"Oh, fuck." Lee's eyes went wide and he gasped, unprepared for the onslaught. He petted Joey's hair with one hand and held on tight to the arm rest on the door with the other. He'd been hard—kissing Joey tended to do that to him—but suddenly he was desperately, completely rigid. Joey's enthusiasm appeared to be undimmed by cramped quarters, the possibility of arrest, or invoking Tony's wrath.

Lee suspected that Tony's wrath wasn't really a concern. He certainly wasn't bothered by it, not with Joey's mouth hot on him and Joey's hands petting Lee's thighs, urging him to spread wider, sprawl deeper.

He looked out the window, a quick glance to make sure no one was coming near them, and then Lee thrust up a little, his hips twitching. Joey moaned and bobbed his head faster, swallowing around him. It made Lee shudder, and the memory of the way Joey had let him fuck that pretty mouth made Lee groan. He couldn't get enough traction to do that, and the angle was all wrong, but Joey was doing all he could to duplicate the experience.

Joey licked and slurped and sucked him, fingers cupping Lee's balls and pressing along the seam of Lee's trousers, rubbing at all the right places. He made noises, enough noises that Lee looked out the window, afraid that a passerby would hear. Not that Lee would stop just because someone would hear.

"God, yes," Lee whispered, his hand in Joey's hair. "Almost." Almost there, almost perfect, almost everything. Lee couldn't concentrate well enough to gather his thoughts into a coherent sentence; one word was about all he could manage. And still Joey worked him, hands and mouth, and then he was sucking only on the head of Lee's cock and there was a storm building inside Lee's brain. "Oh, God!"

When he came it was with a bright burst, hard and fast and sharp, one hand pushing Joey down as his hips snapped up. Joey took it, swallowing around him and licking frantically, wiggling in his seat and rubbing at Lee wherever he could reach. Lee stared out the front window, not seeing anything at all.

"Oh, shit." Joey was panting against Lee's skin, one hand scrabbling at the glove box. "No, no, no—"

"Oh, man." Lee tried to help, yanking the glove box open and pulling out handfuls of napkins as Joey tore his pants open and fought with his belt. "Here!"

"Shit!" Joey grabbed the tissues and fell back awkwardly against Lee's arm as he came, his hands shoved into his trousers. "God damn it."

Lee chuckled and kissed his temple. "Honey. It's okay. I'll take proper care of you back at the hotel, all right?" He was still trying to catch his breath.

"Damn right you will." Joey was panting, too, his face flaming. "For this, I get to top."

Lee's cock twitched. "Uh-huh. You do. Come on, let's get back there and find out who gets to switch rooms with me." He kissed Joey again, tasting himself. "I love you," he said softly. It wasn't scary to say, which was more of a surprise to him than anything else.

Joey smiled and nodded once, slowly. "I love you, too. Let's go and tell your Senior. He'll be pleased that someone's going to take care of you, I think."

Lee laughed. "You know he's going to be keeping tabs on us, right?"

"Oh, I know. And Echo will be just as bad."

"Love them."

Joey smiled and nodded. "Family. It's a good thing to have. And chosen family is even better."

"Our chosen family is going to lecture us when we get to the bar."

"Yeah. We should probably hurry up and let them," Joey said, not rushing to do anything but kiss Lee again.

Sure enough, when they walked into the hotel bar, they were immediately spotted by Tony.

"Where the hell have you—" He blinked and peered

more closely at them. "Oh. You could have called. God."

Lee grinned at him and waved at Carrigan, who was once more playing piano for Matt. "How long has Matt been singing?"

"Not long. He only sings when he takes a break from flirting." Tony looked at Joey and lifted his chin. "Echo's at the bar; he said he's packed but if you didn't show up by the time he had five drinks you'd just have to deal with his drunken ass instead of having a very nice room for your love nest."

Joey looked at the bar and then back at Tony. "He said 'love nest'? Is he already drunk?"

"He's getting close. You two took your time," Tony said reproachfully. "I trust, however, that all is well?"

Lee grinned more widely. "Tell Matt I'll see him in the morning."

Tony nodded. "Breakfast reservation is for nine-thirty. All of us, okay?"

"Sure." Lee leaned over and kissed Tony's cheek. "Good night, Tony."

"Don't make anyone call the front desk to complain about the noise."

Joey laughed and shook his head as he walked away, toward the bar.

"We wouldn't do that," Lee said primly.

"Scout. You two just got off in a car. I think that speaks volumes about what you will and won't do."

To Lee's dismay, he blushed.

Joey fetched Echo and a bottle of wine, and five minutes later Echo's things were in Matt's room, key cards had been exchanged, and the door was closing on a King Suite.

"I think Echo is doing well for himself in theater," Lee said, looking at the large room. "Wow."

Joey smiled but didn't say anything about Lee's first impressions being tied to how much the room cost. "Enjoy it. That bed better be worth it."

"Since you're already undressing, I can pretty much promise the bed will be worth switching rooms." Lee watched as Joey shed his shoes, jacket and tie. "I don't suppose you actually came prepared for sex, did you? I didn't, since you were going to be at home."

Joey smiled at him and looked at the duffle bag he'd brought in from his car. "I knew you were here," he said simply.

Lee nodded and walked to him. "Let me help you with the buttons." His fingers started at the bottom of Joey's shirt and Joey worked them from the top. When they met in the middle there was a pause to kiss for a while, and then the disrobing continued.

Lee's jacket. Two shirts, two belts, trousers. Socks and boxers, and Lee let Joey urge him to the bed, waited while they removed extra pillows and pulled the top covers down.

When Joey finally pushed Lee back onto the bed and hovered over him, Joey's weight balanced on his hands and one knee on the bed, Lee had nothing to do but to look into his eyes and try to breathe. "You're so beautiful," Lee whispered. "And I'm so lucky."

Joey smiled at him and kissed his mouth, licking his way through and tasting every bit he could get to, as if he was keeping Lee for a special treat. "Stay here. Just like this," he said, pulling away.

Lee watched Joey go back to his bag, strong legs in need of a tan, hard abs proving he didn't just sit around in the lab, but had a secret addiction to doing crunches, hard erection leading the way to the supplies they needed.

When Joey came back his smile had turned slightly wicked and he crawled onto the bed between Lee's spread thighs. "Where were we?"

"Right about here." Lee brought one leg up, bent at the knee, so he was more open. His hand curled around his own cock and he started stroking lightly, slowly. "I want you."

"You have me." Joey was watching Lee's hand and sitting back on his own heels. "Keep going."

"Not stopping." Lee put on a bit of a show, his hand getting tighter but not speeding up. With his other hand he rolled his balls, and he lifted his hips ever so slightly, watching Joey twitch and start to lick his lips. "Come on, honey. Play with me."

Joey nodded and popped the top of the lube open with a snap. "Keep going," he said again. He poured a tiny bit of lube onto the head of Lee's cock. "More?"

Lee smoothed it all over and nodded. "Just a little bit." When Joey gave him another drop Lee moaned softly and started jacking off properly.

Joey watched, his eyes dilating, and got a condom open. "That's so sexy," he said, rolling it onto himself. He lubed his fingers and wet Lee's hole. "Try not to come, okay?"

Lee nodded, his eyes closing. "I won't." He was good for a while. Joey's fingers felt good, though, cool and slippery as they slid around over his ass and balls. He lengthened his strokes, his wrist twisting at the head.

"Ohh." Joey seemed to like that, and he eased fingers into Lee's ass, nice and slow. "Again."

Lee did it again, his breathing speeding as his body opened. Joey was going far too slow, teasing. Lee tried to rock down onto his hand, but Joey merely backed off, his fingers not going any deeper until Lee whimpered. Then they stabbed in and rubbed over Lee's gland, twice. "Yes!"

A kiss was pressed to the center of Lee's chest and he

opened his eyes. "Joey."

"Love you."

Lee looked at his eyes, such a pretty brown, and nodded. "I love you. Love me."

Joey's fingers moved, opening him properly, stretching and gliding so sweetly that Lee had to stop playing with his cock or he'd get too close to coming. He wanted to have Joey inside him when he got off, wanted to bring Joey with him.

"Ready?"

"God, yes. Please." Lee heard the thread of need in his voice and wanted to blush for it, but he was too busy lifting his legs to Joey's shoulders and baring his body to really care.

Joey's fingers were gone and Lee's ass was tender, wanting; when the head of Joey's cock pressed in, Lee rocked up, hard. "Oh, yes."

"Lee!" Joey's eyes went wide. "Don't—"

"Yes!" Lee rocked again, greedy for it.

Joey growled and his eyes narrowed. "All right, then."

Grinning, Lee tried to push his advantage a third time, but hands were clamped on his hips, keeping him pinned to the bed. "Oh, oh."

"Right. Oh, oh." Joey pulled back, almost out and slammed back into him. It took three hard thrusts before he found what he was aiming for, but after the first yell he nailed it again and again.

Joey fucked Lee quickly, his strokes long, and deep, and relentless. His cock only seemed to get harder every time Lee swore, gasped or grunted, and he leaned forward, bending Lee even more and getting an even better angle. Lee's cock was trapped between them, and his balls started to ache.

"You first," Joey said between panted breaths. His

eyes were dilated, almost drugged looking, and his thrusts were getting erratic. "Come for me."

Lee nodded, unable to speak as Joey hammered into him. His whole body was lighting up, tingling, and the tension was building to an unbelievable level. All he needed was one more hard thrust—

"I want to feel your ass squeezing my dick."

—and he was coming, pulsing and shaking, his cock throbbing and his ass clamping down on the thick rod in his body.

"Lee!" Joey's back arched and he fucked Lee through his orgasm before freezing, coming hard enough that Lee could feel his cock twitching as he went.

It was minutes before they could speak, and longer before they could do anything more than a cursory clean up. Lee thought he saw Joey's legs wobble as he tried to walk to the bathroom.

When the front desk called to ask them to keep it down, they were suitably contrite. And smug.

Epilogue
Acquired Tastes

One Year Later

"You chose this place?" Tony looked around at the deli and then at Lee. "I would have thought that Dr. Sutton would want something a little more upscale."

"Dr. Sutton has had a year of personal growth." Lee grinned at him and led Tony to the counter. "Try the chicken salad; it's amazing."

Tony nodded and dutifully ordered the chicken salad. "How come you're not going to the graduation ceremony?"

"Because I won't be in the country." Lee ordered as well, and they moved down the line to where they could get their drinks. "I'll be in Bosnia."

Tony was staring at him and it was all that Lee could do to keep from wiggling with glee. "Bosnia. What does Joey think of that?"

"Joey is lamenting his lonely bed for the month I'll be gone. Secretly, I think he's excited about all the free time he's going to have to read trashy novels, but he's not saying that. He's too busy eyeing the way the new

223

maintenance guy doesn't edge the yard properly. I give it another eight months and he'll say something about it."

"You're going to sweep in and say something before then, right?"

"Oh, God, yes. Tomorrow, if I see the guy. It's my duty." Lee let Tony pay, because it was what Tony wanted. This was the lunch to celebrate Lee's doctorate, after all.

"Good." They walked to a table and sat down, and Tony gave him a long look. "You look disgustingly happy," he finally said. "I think I want photos of it."

Lee laughed. "I am. God, I am. I'm done with school, I have a job at Legacy, I get to go to Europe to work and research. Joey and I are talking about getting a dog. Kind of practice, maybe."

"Practice?" Tony froze with a cup halfway to his open mouth. "For what?"

"For babies, of course. We're going to be uncles again. Sometime next year." He loved doing that to people. Matt had hit him, though.

"You're very mean."

"Yeah." Lee smiled. "I am. Hey, Tony?"

"Mmm."

"Thank you. For my life."

Tony looked at him, his eyes growing misty. "Thanks for being you, Lee."

"I'm an acquired taste," Lee said with a slight shrug. "But I'm okay with that. I'm just grateful that you and Joey and Matt love me and took the time to see past the bullshit."

"There's a reason bitter goes with sweet. It makes the sweet that much better." Tony leaned across the tiny table in the crowded deli and kissed him lightly on the lips. "Congratulations, Dr. Sutton. You've made your life yours, on your terms."

Lee nodded. "TCF taught me the terms and you gave

me what I needed. I'm living a life of gratitude, man."

"That's what the world needs." Tony took a huge bite of his chicken salad. "And more of this. Oh, my God."

"I know, right? It's awesome." Lee beamed at him and ate his own lunch, content.

He wanted for nothing other than a puppy, and that would happen after Bosnia. His family would be complete, and Lee Sutton would move forward, as always, acquiring more tastes and never alone.

End

Acquired Tastes

CPSIA information can be obtained at www.ICGtesting.com
261112BV00010B/7/P